KINSMAN AVENUE PUBLISHING, INC.
www.kinsmanquarterly.org

Registered with the U.S. Library of Congress

Printed in the United States of America

Native Voices II: The Cry of Creation

Cover design by Monique Franz

Senior Editor: Monique Franz
Assistant Editing Team: Sophia O. Ofuokwu, Tammy A. Sincavage, Jack Wolflink, Zoe Mares, Shelby Young, and Gabriel Delgado-Cheers.

Contributing Indigenous authors:

Aishik Chakma, Alysha Brooks, Brian Jose Welch, Chang Shih Yen, Douglas Perenara Johnston, D.W. Simerly, Elaine Joy E. Degale, Hannan Khan, Isha Jain, Jay D. Falcetti, Jordan Maison, Kirby Wright, Marc Apilado, Mike Ekunno, N.O. Gomez Flores, Sarah Martinez, Sherry Caayupan, Solape Adetutu Adeyemi, Tommy Cheis, and Vernica Goel.

Photography:
Bamboo photo by Thomas Franz; Bryce Canyon of Utah photo by Sean Pavone; Cook Islands photo by Michael DeFreitas/Danita Delimont; beach shore photo by Angelica Maria; African tree photo by K. Nelson.

Native Voices

The Cry of Creation

Edited by Monique Franz

An anthology of prose and poetry featuring Indigenous voices

Special Thanks

We wish to thank "Brotha" Tim Jones of the Seminole Tribe, the first judge of this annual award for Indigenous writers.
We are grateful for his continued support and sponsorship of Kinsman Quarterly and its underrepresented voices.
We further extend our gratitude to Dr. Deidra Suwanee Dees, a member of the Mvskoke Nation, for serving as selecting judge for the top entries of the 2025 Native Voices Award, whose selected writers are featured in this anthology.

Voices of Asia

Isn't Cooked is Cursed (poetry) by Hannan Khan 1
Ajji's Pineapple Cake (fiction) by Isha Jain 11
Two Sarawakian Poems (poetry) by Chang Shih Yen 19
Silent Struggle (nonfiction) by Vernica Goel 23
The Last Thread (fiction) by Aishik Chakma 27
Heaven's Lips (poetry) by Sherry Caayupan 31
Refreshment (nonfiction) by Marc Andrew Apilado 33
Moonflower (fiction) by Elaine Joy E. Degale 37

Voices of the Pacific Islands

Māmalahoa: Law of the Splintered Paddle (fiction)
by Kirby Wright 51
A Dinner Engagement with Mister Top Hat (fiction)
by Douglas Perenara Johnston 55
*Ram Raid (*fiction) by Douglas Perenara Johnston 63

Voices of the Americas

Lincoyer (historical fiction) by D.W. Simerly 73

A Nationless People (poetry) by Alysha Brooks 77

Howl at the Moon (fiction) by Jordan Maison 85

The Memories of a Non-Rez Kid (poetry) by Sarah Martinez 97

Inheriting Fear (nonfiction) by Jay D. Falcetti 105

Creator Will Never Tell (fiction) by Tommy Cheis 111

Voices of the Caribbean

Dark Moon (poetry) by Brian Jose Welch 131

The Second First Woman (fiction) by N.O. Gomez Flores 135

Voices of Africa

The Heirloom (poetry) by Solape Adetutu Adeyemi 145

The Adventures of Tom the Terror (fiction) by Mike Ekunno 159

Meet the Authors 173

Voices of Asia

Isn't Cooked is Cursed

Hannan Khan

halwa for hymen

your trauma isn't breakfast
but still, they crave you to knead it
hammer it round, hammer it soft, hammer it rise
the kitchen transpires as your therapist
but it doesn't howl questions
only sculpts burns, the gas hisses like gossip
the rolling pin doesn't roll back time
they roar: inherit to cook, inherit to tarry, inherit to swallow
you murmur nothing
you chew your muted glossa
he grazed you; you whispered her, she slapped and bashed you
she bellowed: let him drift away
forget it, forget yourself

every flame in this haven fathoms your shame
every plate clinks with hushedness
every mirror reflects a face that isn't you
but you hold on staring
and it holds on staring back
they pray while you bleed, they savour while you flinch
they fast while you faint
because a girl's honour isn't her veracity
her veracity isn't her body
her clayed body isn't her own
but still — she has to knead, has to roll, has to rise
not for her contusions' rehabilitation but for her wedding night
a raita of abashment, a naan of nerves
halwa for hymen, kheer for keeping quiet
you broke down, so they engineered you a dowry
you implored for therapy, they booked a beauty parlour

you beseeched for healing; they handed you henna
what isn't mouthed is cooked; what isn't cooked is cursed
what is cursed is married; what is married is choked off

your assault isn't morning meal, but you cater it every aurora
with a grin, they tattooed on your mouth
because beti, you have to mold it round,
have to mold it soft, have to mold it rise
and you never have to fish for why

we grade each and everything here

good morning, children
poise in line, don't whisper, whisper in line, don't stand out
lace your shoes, tether your tongues
don't scream, don't shout, don't feel

today we master:
how to enumerate gpa while lusting the grave
how to spell 'perfection' with a razor blade
how to pass without passing out
how to grin while perishing inside
how to perish while grinning outside

you'll memorize:
that a skirt one inch too high is a wickedness
that a boy who cries is weak
that love is grimy, crave is filth
that textbooks matter but therapy doesn't
that silence is an obligatory subject and you better ace it

Islamiyat:
recite verses like bullets, don't probe the trigger
heaven is for the obedient
girls? veil your vices in white
don't ask why Adam sinned—just don't be Eve
hell is ritual, hell is repetition, hell is you
your gasp is weighed, your body? already guilty

Urdu:
we peruse Ghalib, but not fathom him
pen essays on sacrifice while slicing your tongue
poetry bleeds, but yours have to dry
every amour slaughters in a funeral
your metaphors and similes are censored, your utterances, sterilized

Biology:
we silhouette the body, a crime scene
reproduction without pleasure, orgasm without cite
we quote the penis, never tutor of want
the clitoris? doesn't nestle here
hearts beat, but we only gauge pulse
desire is dissected, not discussed

today's homework:
script an essay on 'my aim in life' while
suppressing your panic attacks
ingrain formulas, forget yourself,
lodge before 8 am, don't lodge to your sadness
assembly dismissed; now pray, pray to please,
pray to pass, pray for slumber
pray for muteness, pray to not rouse up tomorrow
or worse—wake up the same

postscript (not for marks):
if you ever jot down a suicide note, make sure it's grammatically
neat and clean handwriting, proper punctuation
we grade each and everything here
even the end too

no one eyes the bloody bird stay

they perched like wailers donned in tar;
tarrying for the vows to putrefy into fruits
a garland drops; its marigold fissures like yolks;
staining dulha's *khussa* with saffron defeat
the dulhan's bangle rattle—not euphoria,
but like chains laboring to reminisce freedom,
she guffaws too wide—lipstick smeared
like a crime vignette still under sleuthing,
his hands tremble over hers as if grazing a curse he can't return;
a scion flings rice,
but the crows cascade faster, more voracious,
sanctified in their ruin; the qazi recites aliases,
neither paramour perceives;
lexemes like rusted nails through tradition; the dhol drowns out
her mom's screams;
embroidered into rhythm like borrowed breath;
a sable crow plucks a cerise *gulab*
from her hair—flies off with what was absquatulated of her girlhood
no one grasps dulha's flinch when the bloody bird lands on his shoulder
and doesn't sway away.

a cactus festered from amour

i sprouted in a terracotta womb
not a verdant garden; not a cradling mom
just cracked clay and assumptions
shemesh baciato me like paramours used to
with lustful interest and then hateful indifference
you were the sultry monsoon: torrential, dramatic
landing only when i had engineered to be alone
you murmured, "let me soften you"
"don't be so prickly, darling," "you crave rough, don't you?"

so, i blistered; moulded into drenched dirt and trembling
no one tutored me how a cactus festers from amour
spoils from your spit smeared like promises between my areoles

i stripped spines like secrets in the bathtub
you brand it intimacy—i marked it decay
we banged like thunderstorms—sizzling, slick with flashbacks
you munched my chlorophylls, tagged them kinks
absquatulate bruises like sticky notes—*mine*
"still hankering," "that's cute"

every moan was a red flag
every "yes" half-wrung from larynx, too tarried to scream
every penance, a yellow flower shoved in my incisors
until i couldn't expectorate
you watered me with guilt—tattooed it care
imprinted it foreplay, engraved it my fault
you dripped apologies like kerosine
and lit them with your seething glossa
you poured into my roots; deserted your perfume like territory
and nourished a whole orchard of ghosts that roared in my slumber

they're mushrooms now, fleshy, obscene
sprawled from the places where your teeth mistook for tenderness
they blossom in rings, sour with sweat
a fungal fuck—you carved into my dermis
you mouthed, "don't sculpt this into a big deal" as i vomited roots
when i finally dried up, smashed open like dreadful fruit
all pulp metamorphosed into acrid
you stamped me selfish, "you're no fun when you don't implore"
"you were better broken," "you savoured it, feasted it"
"you longed for this, all of it"

your soaked chorus still clung to my bones
like perspiration in unwashed sheets
now i photosynthesize spite—i penetrate the sol with my naked skin
let it shoot aurum into my scars; i bloom in filth i forelsket
and i'm erected again, even in *mallëngjim*
when no one's ardently eyeing

men who bawl like mountains

he woke at five, trimmed silence off his face, wore arrears as dermis
each bill he graved in his side drawer mushroomed like mountains

he pined for his abba at the wedding, not the hombre, but the voidness
the grin he donned fissured under heftiness and parched like mountains

no room to drift apart at work, no lacrima ventured to cross his eye
so hearty laughter morphed into a mask he leashed like mountains

he was wired to bleed in colorless nooks,
then sculptured the nooks his contusions
a ferocious fist metamorphosed into his lullaby;
he perished within like mountains

she whispered *don't be soft*,
so he smashed his softness into fervent knives
he clenched his jaw 'til tenderness ripped
his pride and esteem like mountains

he devoured war to raise his son;
the son raised war in the man who devoured
the bed was engineered with quietude and salt;
both busted him wide like mountains

his munchkin whistled, "do men bawl too?' he sighed,
"in slumber, sometimes"
he kissed his little one,
then gulped the timeless truth and lamented like mountains

he hauled funerals in his cracking bones,
but never voiced their sweet cognomens
grief and saudade weren't manly,
so he pleated sprawling pain inside like mountains

the exercise, the namaz mat,
the bottle—all hammered into small escapes
he choked each scream into a bench press
and then lied like mountains

he learned to fear the boy in him, so he engraved him in games
then implored that boy to come back and slide like mountains

oh Hannan, ardently pen him brave, but not so brave he shatters alone
breath, god still bends towards those men who bawled like mountains

Ajji's Pineapple Cake

Isha Jain

Ajji's home always smelled sweet, especially in the mornings. It was a sharp contrast to the warm buttery smell from Ajjo's bakery in front of their home.

Ajjo made me pack the breads, muffins and the few pastries he made for the customers in the mornings when I ran to him after the forced bath. My feet dangled from his chair behind the counter as he passed me the orders to be kept in the jute bags the regulars bought. They spent time sitting on the mismatched tables Ajjo would get from the second-hand shop in town while they waited for me.

I loved helping him out at the busiest time of the day. But it was their garden in the middle where I spent most of my summer vacations.

The heat didn't bother us there like it did back in Bombay. One could lie in the front grass all day, and feel full from just the heady mix of aroma. Maa often joked that her parents were in a competition with each other to make the locals fatter.

No one served a pineapple cake like my Ajji. She made everything the best in the world, but the cake was my favourite. I only learned later on that she only baked it for special occasions. Festivals, birth of a child, marriage ceremonies, or the woman's monthly meetings at the local café. It was the highlight of any gathering. All parties thrown by the neighbours were crowded by relatives who had the cake once and would never miss the chance again.

Yet, there was always one in their fridge to be served after meals when we went over for vacations. The locals loved that they could drop by anytime and have a piece. I might have gotten many candies for being the reason of sweet treat.

But Ajji never made the cake to sell it at the bakery along with other treats Ajjo made, "They would not ask for anything else but this, then." She had winked at me while mixing the flour once as her husband shouted from the other room.

"I heard that." It made her laugh.

Ajji didn't mind baking another one in the evening if we ran out as Mama stood by her side to learn, losing interest soon enough and preparing dinner instead.

Once I was old enough, Ajji let me help, in mixing the flour and eggs while she cut the fruit on her own. I did my best but Maa laughed when she had to do it herself, shooing me off to join Ajjo on the dining table.

Maa tried it every year for my birthday when I begged. It didn't taste the same. So, we started ordering from different bakeries for occasions. The search didn't stop there. Whenever we went to any place that served the cake, we ordered the fruity one and compared it to the best, never finding any that could come close.

Maa said it's because they used canned pineapples. It made the cake sweeter, loosing that fresh tart taste in Ajji's.

I would nod, pretending to attend the technical difference. But I knew it was something else. They didn't serve it in the steel plate like Ajji, with the small spoon she would have to fish in the drawer for. They either used paper or fancy plates.

Their cake pieces were always perfect rectangles too, not triangle, a messy square, a serving of spoonfuls, or sometimes a circle Ajji would cut in the middle for me with the ice cream scooper she had purchased when I was ten, "It will taste the best." She told me.

Sometimes, my friends went with me just because they had heard so much about the cake and wanted to taste it themselves. I beamed when they took their first bite and moaned, always asking for another piece and reluctant to go back to their own Granny's house. And I knew it was because of the cake, not only the creek we swam in, or the library and theatre we visited in the evenings.

Ajji would pack them a whole cake for their family. I knew it would never reach that far. Maa and I barely left any for Appa whenever she gave us one for the trip.

Ajjo also had fun in telling the few boys that I bought over, how the temperature of his oven could even burn human fingers. Ajji would roll her eyes before swatting at his hand while Maa would hum along, sipping her juice like I had seen people do in the movies from their big glasses. The police inspector uncle often visited for dinner during those summer vacations till I stopped bringing any of my male friends along.

I went alone, and I refused to go back with Maa till she had no choice but to leave me for a week more. She would pick up my homework from the school so that I could rush through it in one night, and drop off an application.

Ajjo made the trip to drop me back safely in the bus and went back the same night to open his bakery the next morning. I know Maa hated coming back to Mumbai too, especially after Appa left us.

Ajji and Ajjo had come to our flat for the first time then. I had given up my room for them. It was smaller than their kitchen, but they hardly slept for those two days, going back the evening we came back from church.

From that summer, Maa could only drop me at Ajji's house, going back the same night to work the next day. It was the first time I had heard her raise her voice, "You know I have to pay the debt first! And, I can't drag her here with me." Why? I wanted to ask her. I would have loved to live forever with Ajji and Ajjo. She didn't agree with me.

So, when Maa decided to move back to her hometown when I turned eighteen, Ajji and Ajjo threw a party. She made dozens of cakes till it seemed like the locals were more drunk on the sweets than the beer served to them.

Only I was the sad one at the celebration, and refused to eat anything. It was unfair that Maa was coming here when I had to stay in a hostel for college. She wanted me to go out of the country and settle in a foreign land while she would help Ajjo run the bakery.

No amount of screaming, begging or getting Ajji to talk to her made her change her mind. I had thought of a compromise by applying to the University closer to them. She tore that off and enrolled me herself in a marketing course away, beyond the seas.

I did as she wanted. I went and got a degree. I got a job I never liked. And I earned more than I would require back in India for long.

But for seven years, I didn't step a foot in Goa. I didn't even taste any cake. I only came back with an idea that was turned down without a second thought by her.

Ajji's cake could go global, or at least create a wave at the national level. But Maa wouldn't even let me take it to the bakeries of mainland Goa. She asked me to never mention it to her mother. I had stomped my foot and rushed off the dining table.

I had cried that evening in the garden, thinking myself a wronged heroine of movies that Ajji loved when she served a piece to me. My first after years, and too much to be eaten at one go.

There were more wrinkles around her eyes than I remembered. The sun had left its red spots on her hands too. But the cake remained the same as I gobbled it down between hiccups till she had to pat my back.

She had smiled as she sat down with me on the ground, starting with how I couldn't even tell the difference between a good and bad one as long as she made it. No local could. How she used to experiment a lot whenever I came over, changed the recipe a thousand times to see if I stopped liking the cake one day. How Maa had lost many bets over the years when Ajji served me a cake that Maa would have made the night before and I still wouldn't complain.

Maa just shook her head at me and told her to tell me the story. Ajji's whole body jiggled with laughter as she told me a time when she had run out of pineapples. She had mixed a variety of fruits to get the flavour as close as possible and I hadn't even noticed while I ate it in front of the television while Ajjo was braiding my hair.

My eyes widened. I didn't remember that ever happening. I had always loved her pineapple cake to the point I didn't eat any other kind.

Ajjo also joined us on the ground, bidding goodbye to the last customers, wiping his hands on the shirt which Ajji dusted off lovingly while he laughed about the time he had tried to change the recipe at his bakery. The locals had made it very clear that they could not be fooled with their bread and had to be quietened down by sweet bribes from the lady of the house.

Maa also told me stories of introducing new kinds of breads she had been trying to experiment with at the bakery. The locals would only try it if Ajji came and handed it out for free to try it once. They were just coming around to demanding Maa's stuff before Ajjo's, especially the younger customers.

"It is never about what you are serving to people, it is about who and why." Ajji patted my hand.

Ajjo invited me to work with him that night, if I wanted, to stop my tears. Not like I had any choice, I had told them between sniffles, making them laugh. I had quit my job because I wanted to come back home and starting the business had felt like the right reason.

It took me months to learn all his and Maa's recipes. I never talked about my idea again, even when people came from faraway places to eat at our small bakery, and asked if we had any branches. I only smiled and pointed to the "since 1962, one and only" sign Ajjo had put when he opened the bakery. They made videos, clicked pictures and got our stuff packed, in dozens, especially during tourist seasons.

In other months, locals were our regular customers, trying every new thing and being the first judge of a dish that could be added to the menu or not.

I also tried with some things of my own, adding a coffee bar and some fresh lemon drinks since I was mostly given accounting work while Ajjo and Maa handled cooking and baking for most of the time.

Till Ajji came to the bakery one day. It was a slow day, and Ajjo and Maa had gone to the market.

Ajji didn't say anything. She started making her cake from the scratch till I began helping her as old songs played from the radio Ajjo had installed in the back. By the evening, we had half a dozen cakes cooling in our display.

When the friends I had made locally came to pick me up for a movie, they stopped to buy the treats. Ajji looked at me with a small smile when I shook my head and declared they were not for sale.

She got up to serve them their slices as the small space started filling with people who could smell the sweet scent from the street.

Ajjo and Maa had come back when we were on our last two, surprised at the loud crowd and taking over the serving duties from us.

Ajji came and sat at my table with her own, enjoying a piece from the cake that I had made.

I grinned, stealing some from her plate.

Two Sarawakian Poems

Chang Shih Yen

Gadong Bumi Kamek

Translated as "green is my land" in Bahasa Sarawak, the local Malay dialect of the state of Sarawak.

My land is so green,
dark green as the rainforest.
The sigh of the wind
rustles the emerald green leaves,
the susurration of the trees,
as the gentle zephyr blows,
sending its whispers to the mountain,
lush and fertile green.
The blue of the sky,
beauty to my eye.
Wind, send my regards
to the foothills of the mountain.
Let the waters of the mighty Rajang flow,
my melancholy to be foam
on the lonely sea.

I Am More Than A Box Called "Other"

In Malaysia, the forms list the main ethnic groups along with a box called dan lain-lain (and others). In the state of Sarawak, Indigenous people are lumped into this one box although they make up the population's majority, having at least 26 ethnic groups, each with their own language, some reflected in this poem.

Fill in this form? Yes.
Sure. Name, address?
No problem.
Now, we come to race,
Hmmm… Malay? Chinese? Indian?
No, that's not me.
That only leaves *dan lain-lain.*
Other.
Where's my box?
I am more than a box called 'other.'
Bansa Iban, ngelaban! Iban people, fight!
Rise up, show our might.
Diki bangsa Bidayuh? Where's the Bidayuh people?
We deserve our own box.
Ko eh bangsa Melanau. I am Melanau.
Give me a box to tick now.
Akui anak Kayan. I am Kayan.
Acknowledge me.
Ake' du Kenyah. I am Kenyah.
I am here.
Uih Kelabit. I am Kelabit.
I exist.
Weh Lun Bawang. I am Lun Bawang.
Hear my voice.

I am Lun Dayeh. I am Kajang.
I am Sihan.
See me.
I am Kejaman. I am Lahanan.
Hear me.
I am Ukit.
Recognize me.
I am Berawan,
Don't forget me.
Please don't confuse Penan
with Punan.
We are different people.
Know me.
Stand up. We are here.
At least give me a box to tick.
A box that's more than *dan lain-lain.*
Kamek anak Sarawak. We are Sarawakians.
We deserve so much more.

Silent Struggle

Vernica Goel

Vernica Goel

With a broom in one hand and a mop in the other, I scrub the marble floors of glass towers, imagining my children someday sitting inside, not as cleaners, but as executives tapping away on laptops that cost more than I earn in a year.

With blistered palms and a sunburned back, I mold bricks and stack dreams at kilns, hoping the foundations I lay today will house my descendants tomorrow—seven generations later, perhaps, when we finally break free from this vicious circle of poverty we currently live in.

With bare hands, I gather the remains of animals struck by cars so luxurious I can't even pronounce their names, silently wishing that my bloodline might one day drive one, even as the chauffeur.

With a few cuts on my fingers and a thousand more on my soul, I stitch leather into luxury. I build beautiful masterpieces for the high-and-mighty who haggle over pennies but never question the price of their pride.

And with the rough, calloused palms of an honest worker, I join my hands in prayer, bowing to plead, asking for nothing more than a roof over my head, clothes on my bruised skin, and a meal to make it to morning.

Dalit (the lowest stratum of the castes in India)

India is a Sovereign Socialist Secular Democratic Republic Nation, whose constitution was written by Dr. B.R. Ambedkar, a Dalit himself, who would be rolling in his grave if he saw how heartlessly his countrymen treat his community even today.

Sadness hits you when you discover the caste-based discrimination and violence prevalent in every nook and cranny. Rage surrounds you when you realise that the Dalit community is not only discriminated against but also struggles to meet its basic human rights. It has been over 75 years since India received independence, yet this community is fighting to keep its identity and fulfil its daily necessities that we, the privileged ones, take for granted every day.

When someone experiences such brutality on a daily basis, as this community does, one would only assume that they would look for violent means to express their rage. However, they use harmless and peaceful methods to bind their community. They sing songs about their leader, B.R. Ambedkar, and the values he stood for. They remember his contributions, principles, and vision of social equity in Indian society. Dalits are not the blind disciples of Ambedkar but his sincere followers. They celebrate his birth as a reminder of what a person with a vision can achieve regardless of caste. Celebrating Ambedkar Jayanti is a statement and representation of pride amongst the people of the Dalit community.

When arguably the most oppressed community (Dalits) in the country tried to show their pride by protesting for what they believed in, the privileged oppressors (police) came in to show their strength. We see a show of power in the worst form of violence by the team led by a man with a seat of power, who gave the order to open fire on these defenceless men. His utter arrogance was fueled by the unjust hatred he had for the Dalit community. Every person who engaged in the violence that day, responsible for killing ten unarmed, harmless humans, cannot take pride in their actions. All they can do is regret their actions and reflect on the consequences that followed.

The police officers take pride in carrying a gun and a badge that gives them a license to kill if necessary, and they failed miserably in their duty that day. Moreover, they will keep failing until and unless there is a radical change in people's mindsets. A change that allows us to value people for who they are and what they do instead of where they come from. Every time a person stands up for who they are, truthfully, they display the pride within them.

We believe that we need to eradicate the caste system from our society. But we must realise that a system that came about thousands of years ago will not go away in a day or a year. Hence, we need to eradicate caste-based discrimination and violence from our hearts first, and then from our society. Saying that we are a secular society is not enough; we have to show through our actions that we believe in it and that we are not afraid of practising equality, liberty, and fraternity—the pillars of the foundation of our republic that Dr B.R. Ambedkar envisioned.

In a world that prides itself on progress, we stand as witnesses to the weight of an ancient, oppressive system anchoring millions to the depths of despair. The Dalit community, with its unyielding spirit, stands as a testament to resilience against a society that denies them the dignity they deserve. Yet, their story is not merely one of silent suffering—it is a story of hope, songs sung in reverence, and dreams that refuse to be extinguished.

The battle to dismantle caste-based discrimination is not a sprint but a marathon, requiring collective action, introspection, and unwavering courage. The question is not whether change is possible—it is whether we, as a society, are brave enough to rise to the occasion and carve out a future where humanity triumphs over a thousand-year-old hierarchy. After all, if the world has to (r)evolve, we need to smoothen the rough edges surrounding prejudice, caste discrimination, and violence.

The silent struggle of the Dalit community must no longer echo in empty chambers; it must resound in our classrooms, boardrooms, and courtrooms. Equality isn't a favour to be granted—it's a right long overdue. If Dr. Ambedkar could rise from the deepest margins to draft a nation's conscience, the least we can do is honour his vision by turning empathy into action. Because the real revolution won't begin with raised fists but with open minds, honest hearts, and hands—calloused or smooth—joined in solidarity.

The Last Thread

Aishik Chakma

The loom stopped. Silence filled the bamboo hut like smoke.

Doya, fourteen, stared at her grandmother's hands—still, for the first time in years. The old woman sat hunched, eyes cloudy, the final thread of a red-and-black *pinon* draped across her lap.

"Finish it..." Grandma whispered. "Before they forget."

Outside, the sound of machines echoed from the valley below. The rubber factory had arrived last week—trucks, noise, concrete. Men in dusty helmets had marked the trees with red paint. The forest, once filled with the laughter of monkeys and the smell of ripe jackfruit, was now fenced off with steel.

"But I've never... I only watched you," Doya said, kneeling by her grandmother. "I don't know how."

"You know more than you think. Your fingers remember even when your mind forgets."

Doya looked at her hands, stained with turmeric from helping in the kitchen and chipped from carrying water in steel pitchers down the steep hill. Could these hands carry the memory of her people?

Before the machines came, Doya's world was measured in sunrises over the Karnaphuli and the rhythm of the loom. Her grandmother, Buroi, had woven stories into every thread—not just cloth, but memory: of how her mother once hid in the jungle during the war, of how mangoes tasted sweeter when stolen, of how men used to court women by placing *bajus* around their wrists and songs by moonlight.

Each traditional pattern had a name—*Dhusri*, *Gorh-muri*, or *Tangail-lar*. Not words from textbooks—words born from hands, passed from one generation to the next like prayer.

Now, the village girls wanted jeans. TikTok. Dhaka dreams. Nobody wore traditional *pinon-hadi* unless it was a wedding or a government event. The loom was no longer a necessity. It was a relic.

And yet, Doya found herself threading the needle.

The first row was shaky. The second, slightly better. Buroi coughed beside her, but her eyes followed every movement. "Yes. Like that. Tighter. Not too fast—let it breathe."

“I’m not good at this,” Doya mumbled.

“Neither was I when I started. The threads will forgive you. They are patient.”

Outside, her younger brother ran past the hut with a plastic gun he’d won at the weekly fair. He shouted something in broken Bangla to a friend. Doya winced. When had their mother tongue become so diluted?

She kept weaving.

The *lal chunti*, the deep crimson dye, used in weaving. The black of mourning. The yellow line her grandmother always said was the sun’s promise after rain. Each color meant something—not just aesthetics, but history encoded in warp and weft.

As the cloth grew under her fingers, Doya remembered things. How her grandfather used to dip betel leaf into lime paste with a grin. How the village shaman once danced for three days straight when her cousin fell sick. How the rains came heavy during *Boishakh*, the first month of the Bengali calendar, signifying the new year), flooding the lower bamboo floors.

She remembered her mother’s voice—soft, Chakma lullabies about forest birds and restless rivers.

By midnight, Doya’s fingers were blistered. Her back ached. But the *pinon* was almost done.

Buroi sat silently now. Her eyes were closed, a faint smile on her lips.

“Grandma?” Doya said, softly. “It’s ready.”

She placed the finished piece in Buroi’s lap.

For a moment, there was no response. Then, a slow breath. Eyes opened, glistening.

“Beautiful,” she murmured. “You’ve given me peace.”

The next morning, Buroi was gone — quietly, in her sleep, wrapped in the *pinon* Doya had finished.

They buried her on the hill, where the tamarind tree bent toward the sun. Doya placed the loom near the grave, and the village elders nodded in solemn approval.

Later that week, the factory sent men to mark more land. A government officer offered the villagers a resettlement plan—concrete flats far from the river, near the highway.

"Modern life," he smiled. "Better opportunities."

Doya said nothing. That night, she gathered the girls from the village. In the same hut, under the same flickering kerosene light, she showed them how to weave.

Not for money. Not for tourists. But because some stories must be told without words.

Because a thread, once broken, is hard to repair. Because some cloth holds more than color—it holds soul.

Heaven's Lips

Sherry Caayupan

The lips of heaven break forth
as to enunciate its heavenly ground.
From all walks of which is sky bound,
where I shall wait for its soft sweet whisper.
It shall breathe into unbarren dominion that pours forth—
consecrated words—one hasn't heard of such sweet grace.
For when heaven flutters its beauteous wings,
I shall wait eagerly with a single touch of fling,
even if time would kiss forever or to eternity;
And when by time, heaven foretells my sweet wish
from an undying sweet cherish
of both hearts that listen to heaven's throbbing sweetness...
...the kiss of thine lips shall prove endlessness...
...into sweet, sweet love's undying restlessness.

Refreshment

Marc Andrew Apilado

Which do you prefer on a sizzling July afternoon? Orange juice? Lemonade? Or, if you're fancy enough, sparkling water? Regardless of your choice, each option is inarguably refreshing on a hot summer day. But for a child, there is nothing more refreshing than July afternoons, which are among the best times of the year—no school, no tasks, and complete freedom to play outside. But when shifting perspective to the youth from the year of 2023, does the same refreshment still apply? Do summer afternoons mean anything aside from being off from school?

Among today's technologically infected and culturally bombarded youth, voices can still be heard, though not from them, but rather from those who experienced childhood in the Philippines. A yearning rhythmic noise—a refreshing culture yet to diminish, but nearing its demise. The *tumbang preso*, *mataya taya*, or *sekyo*—among countless games that sometimes involve going home bruised or dirty—the epitome of Filipino youth—*batang pinoy*.

Year 2020 landed a heavy blow on everyone's jaw. The deadly virus suddenly took over the lifestyles people had, bringing an increase to the global mortality rate. It transformed peaceful lives into spaces of new dangers. People sheltered within their homes, minimizing outside contact, and following mandated precautions.

With the isolation and loss of physical connection to loved ones, society became dependent on technology. Work, school, business, shopping—all were accomplished online. Technology played a pivotal role in coping with the situation. Some even became immersed in culture as a result of the internet's widespread information.

Traversing to 2023, everything began reverting back to normal—the pandemic slowly receding. Opportunities reopened, in-person activities resumed, and social distancing prohibitions were discontinued. But are things back to normal?

A few improvements were made—some personal, societal, or even universal. But with nominal enrichment, the pandemic brought decline to the "hope" of the nation, the next in line—the youth.

The pandemic provoked habits within our youth, and not enough light is shed on whether the changes are an improvement. The youth *are* more technologically astute, gaining more access to knowledge. But from a larger perspective, young people are becoming more dependent on their devices, immersed in external cultures presented through their screens.

Youth between 5–10 years old are supposed to develop treasurable memories, but instead, most remain indoors, buried in their rooms, staring at a handheld, radiation-emitting box.

It was once valid to fear the outdoors and the dangers of the pandemic, but we must re-root ourselves in the motherland. Allow children to run free, explore every nook and cranny of our home country, and discover what it takes to be a "batang pinoy."

The world has grown more dangerous, and life must be treasured. This is all the more reason to let children venture outdoors, for youth is but a passing moment. Encourage children to play, for that is what truly refreshes on a hot summer day.

Moonflower

Elaine Joy E. Degale

Under the apricot colors of a bursting dawn, the clouds exhale into the vastness of blue skies as if pushing the colors of dusk down towards the tall palm trees that surround the Edaya farm. Jojo shines her flashlight into the pile of *tsinelas*—flip flops—scattered under the base of her home's entrance. She searches for her yellow pair, but somehow it is gone. She takes her sister's blue pair, and journeys toward the farm animals to feed the hogs and ducks.

The hogs stir about with the urgency of hunger, and their demands grow louder at the sight of their caretaker. Jojo's father, Tomás, is pouring homemade pig-feed made of shredded corn and taro leaves into the hog pans. He greets his favorite daughter good morning, while she pours water into the perforated latex gallons that serve as water cups for the hogs they raise together. Jojo eyes her father's wide feet violating the elasticity of her newly purchased yellow *tsinelas*.

"*Papa naman*, my *tsinelas* are brand new, I bought them a few sizes bigger so they can last longer. They are not gonna last if you keep using them!"

Her father looks at his short, lumpy feet resting upon the grass and briefly contemplates this comment, then laughs loudly at his daughter's audacity. He pulls his feet backwards, squeezing the width of his feet through the narrow opening. After some effort, the yellow *tsinelas* escape the torture with a sigh of relief.

"Hey, are you wearing your sister's *tsinelas*?" he says. "Here, you take these back because I know you bought these yourself, Jojo. Merlyn never buys anything for herself, so since I bought those for her, I offer you here, a fair trade."

Jojo is pleased at this affectation of justice, and merrily trades her sister's old, blue *tsinelas* for her rightfully owned, new yellow *tsinelas*. Her father immediately runs away, and Jojo soon realizes that his 'kind gesture' had alternative motives. She is overwhelmed by the stench of feces coming from the soles of her *tsinelas* where brown, sticky badges of warm justice sit.

"Dadddddd!!!!!" Jojo is beyond herself with anger. Her father is reeling from laughter, far away from Jojo.

He cups his screams with both hands and advises his daughter, "You should always examine all sides of any deal you enter, sweet Jojo! Also, make sure you bathe the hogs! Hahahahaha… and wash your feet!"

Jojo pours water over her feet, and violently skids her yellow *tsinelas* over a green patch of grass. The blob of feces under her soles gradually surrenders to the blades of grass. She returns to the water pump and uses her entire weight to pump water from the underground well. When her bucket overflows, she takes the water to the pig pen and soaps up the rest of the hogs. As she brushes the flank of the third hog, she talks to them about America.

"In America, I wonder if they have pigs like you. I wonder if people there eat *litson* too! Wow, imagine, you, Mr. Piggy, a delicious, tasty meal eaten in a land full of plenty! I hear no one is poor there, in America, and everyone has blue eyes."

The hogs sigh in a sloberry response, squirming at the discomfort of being bathed during a meal. Jojo continues to hum as she bathes them. She keeps distracting the hogs with food as she scrubs their skin until the golden tint of their fur is visible again. On the chopping board, her father has laid out taro leaves and a knife. Jojo cuts as many taro leaves as she can, and dumps the rest of it into a steaming cauldron. The cauldron is an oversized Nabisco tin container, where a bunch of snacks used to live. Now, it is a makeshift cauldron where she stirs hog food over a fire near the lake. Just a typical way of the Filipinos on this side of Mindanao where items are rarely discarded but rather find new functions. A plastic ice cream container, for instance, finds a second life as food storage, and a bean can as a rice scooper in the pantry.

After she makes the hog food reserved for lunchtime, Jojo climbs one of their two *carabaos*—water buffalos—and heads west to find a deeper lake for the animals to bathe in. The *carabao*s have high cultural significance in province states across the Philippines, Malaysia, Indonesia, and Guam. A carabao is heftier than a caribou, and is typically preferred over horses in the provinces in the Philippines for its strength and utility —a staple among farmer families who rely on the carabao to transport harvested rice, corn, and coconuts. You can ride on a carabao's back, or you can use a wooden *carro*, or flatbed carriage, to carry more people across town. The sickle-shaped horns of the carabao, almost symbolize the communist ideologies typically associated with the rural poor. But historically, most Asian nations never deluded themselves with the allure that communism in itself was enough to shape an economy. You will always need capital. It is only the youthful public intellectuals born into exorbitant wealth that championed the fantasy of a communist order that repudiates capitalism.

On January 26, 1954, The Magsaysay administration temporarily outlawed the slaughter of the carabao so that the prices of this staple animal can remain accessible for the rural poor. For us, the carabao was a car, before having a car was possible for the common man in a developing democracy.

Dried patches of mud begin to form like giant saucers of ash printed on the sleek gray skin of the carabaos. As Jojo tries to untangle the ropes that are leashed on the animals, the carabao she's riding on decides to position its backside downwards in a suspicious position.

Jojo slides down the back of the carabao, stumbling into its warm freshly produced goo. Before she has a chance to steady herself on the slippery arch of grass behind the carabao, she's whipped across the face by the carabao's hefty tail, and furiously rolls into the shallow lake. As Jojo tumbles into the lake, she gulps down large amounts of rancid water, and waves her arms in panicked succession like a bullfrog desperately searching for elevated rock. She screams a piercing *Deputa,* which loosely translates to *Curse the Thunder*, as she tries to get back on solid land. After hoisting herself back into the shoulder of the lake, she searches for a long branch to row her floating yellow *tsinelas* back to shore. On retrieval, she examines them to make sure they didn't sustain any cuts from her fall. Understanding that they were the culprit of her fall, she weaves her right arm through both *tsinelas*, opting to go barefoot for the rest of her journey. She climbs on the other *carabao*, who seems oblivious to the whole ordeal. Somehow, this infuriates her even more. Saturated in soiled water and unmitigated wrath, Jojo leads them toward the deeper lake. She attempts to remain calm, but fury has painted the roundness of her cheeks with the undeniable triumph of bloody anger.

Jojo has little patience for the absurd. It occurs to her that these twisted sisters conspired against her—these evil carabaos, both of which she refuses to name because of their natural cruelty toward her. As she rides the back of the carabao, she greets the farmers and family friends who are already knees deep, cultivating the rice fields at the break of dawn.

She cups her voice in her tiny hands, and screams *"Maayong Aga Gid Dira Lola Susan!"*

She delights in herself the feeling of serendipity. Now that she knows Old Susan is out planting rice in the field, there's certainly all the reason to yell the sweetest "Good Morning Old Susan" as she begins to plot a breakfast robbery in Susan's thriving henhouse. As far as Jojo was concerned, this greeting was her way of asking permission to 'borrow' some eggs for her family. Further down the road, she sees her cousin, Reviro 'Beroy' Bunda Esmalana Jr., who is also doing the daily carabao walk. His family only has one carabao. He sees Jojo and her two carabaos, and examines the paleness of her skin, where stubborn mud and vines of ferns and ivy are in rambunctious concert, forming patterns of vengeance across the width of her face, and stretching throughout the length of her arms.

While it is not unusual for Jojo to have the prints of agriculture daintily foisted upon her in curious patterns, today's tumble through the lake has left prominent marks on her. Beroy, bewildered by Jojo's presentation, immediately bursts into laughter. Quickly composing himself at the sight of Jojo's death glare, he relegates his predilections to satisfy the common points of curiosity one attempts to embody in such bizarre situations.

"Noy, what happened to you?"

Still unable to resist the enticement of humor in typical Filipino style, he adds, "You were swimming in the beach, I see." He bites his lower lip to exchange the urge to laugh for a bit of pain. It's the best he could do for his cousin.

Jojo responds with the stare of a tyrant, assessing the adequate punishment of an underling's betrayal. "Don't try it, Beroy."

Beroy knew better than to offend Jojo. All the boys in the neighborhood called Jojo 'Noy'. It was the masculine nickname her dad gave her because he really wanted the second child to be a boy. So far, all his three creations have been girls, and with the birth of Genesis last Christmas, still girls.

Their new neighbor and Jojo's favorite teacher who teaches world history, Sir Joaquín Mendoza Peralejo, happens to pass by, greeting them both with great appreciation.

"*Guten Morgen* to you Mr. Beroy," an air of exaggerated benevolence surrounds him. "Salutations to you as well, Ms. Jocelyn. I see you are both taking great care of your chores and responsibilities this fine early morning. Your parents must be proud."

He extracts an elegant handkerchief from his pocket, stroking away the beads of sweat accumulating across the sharpness of his nose, then swiping across the wide expanse of his forehead. His copper eyes, sunken and bruised from sleepless nights, shine like muted daggers—full of quiet sadness, exhausted secrecy, and a darkness begging to consume the fullness of his humanity. Yet he smiles, especially for his favorite student, Jojo.

"Ms. Jocelyn, congratulations, I've seen a memo circling through faculty chambers. Tiny and terrible, yet top of her class!"

Faculty chambers? Certainly an embellishment given that Jojo is an eight-year-old. Yet exaggeration was the most prominent feature of Sir Joaquín Mendoza Peralejo's character. A visiting teacher and former professor from the prestigious Ateneo De Manila of the Philippines, he piques Jojo's ambitions in many ways. From being a research fellow on a Harvard Scholarship, studying the education system of indigenous agrarian communities, to being the son of descendants of Spanish *encomenderos* who owned massive lands that enslaved many Filipinos until June 12, 1898, when Filipinos declared their independence from Spain. Jojo wasn't envious of this particular history, but of what he does with it, because Sir Joaquín Mendoza Peralejo, haunted by the specter of his family tree, returned down south to serve, and culturally elevate her people. Some strange form of self-guided justice, maybe.

A man of many religions, decorated in many things, always floating through a town that would have never known he was worthy of a second glance if he did not so desperately adorn himself with material symbols of wealth, a speech of flowery language, and a tongue full of worldly idiomatic expressions. He was a male Carmen Sandiego before there was ever such a thing. Sir Joaquín Mendoza Peralejo was, indeed, oh so many things.

To say that Jojo adored this man would be an understatement. It was clear to her that one day she must try to be like him, sans the post-colonial guilt. To Sir Joaquín Mendoza Peralejo's attempt at conversation, Jojo responds with frozen embarrassment, and a silence that is almost unbecoming of her if she was not such an adorable mess of a child dipped in the earlier tragedies of excrement and mud. Sir Joaquín Mendoza Peralejo is accustomed to Jojo's moodiness. Jojo slowly extracts her yellow *tsinelas* off her arm, placing them softly on the toes of both her feet to preserve an ounce of civility despite her current presentation, imagining a moment in another world, where the teacher she respects the most will not remember this moment. She fails to form a response, and softly plops herself face down against the wet shiny back of her carabao, effectively hiding from the embarrassment of the situation.

Out of sight, out of mind.

Sir Joaquín Mendoza Peralejo, rearranges his gold-rimmed spectacles, almost a spitting image of the national hero, José Rizal, and surrounded by a forcefield of expensive cologne. He is holding a briefcase, and Beroy asks, "Where are you headed, Sir Joaquín Mendoza Peralejo? It's Saturday, no?"

Sir Joaquín Mendoza Peralejo responds with a laugh, "Certainly. I have an appointment in Manila, we are working on translating legal cases for children who were—errr—um," he searches his brain for more child-friendly words to describe the plight of children saved from sex tourism industries in the north. "...stolen. Yea, we are setting up to translate legal case files for young girls and boys who were—um, stolen, during the war."

Sir Joaquín Mendoza Peralejo loosens his tie. He was always so uncomfortable to lie, which makes the future events to befall this town become so much more ironic in the years to come.

"Anyhow," he peeks behind the carabao's neck where Jojo buried herself, "I hear you are singing Consuelo Velázquez's *Bésame Mucho* during the Santo Niño Founding Festival? I can't wait to see you shine, Ms. Jocelyn."

Jojo responds with an awkward silence. It must be that this man has yet to understand that she refuses to exist in this moment of her history.

Beroy, realizing that Jojo is in need of some comedic relief, sees the perfect opportunity poking its frayed gray head out of Jojo's hair. He pulls out a dead baby snake out of her hair, "Look," he pushes the dead snake toward her, "did you know this was in your hair?"

Sir Joaquín Mendoza Peralejo takes a step backwards, perplexed by the casual demeanor of a young boy holding a snake, with the same regards to it as he would a fluffy bunny.

"Sir, did you see? Look, it is a snake! In Jojo's hair! Haha!" Beroy's Korean eyes disappear into a lively celebration of humor, his sun-kissed complexion glistening under the spell of amusement.

Sir Joaquín Mendoza Peralejo checks his watch for the time, and excuses himself. Addressing Jojo as he leaves, "Anyhow, as they say in Italian to every beautiful performer, *bocca al lupo,* Ms. Jocelyn." He glances toward Beroy, and bows into an awkward "*Sayonara.*" Sir Joaquín Mendoza Peralejo urgently shuffles himself away, squeezed by the confines of his tailor-made suit, and his disposition that of a man afraid of his own shadow.

Beroy, holding the snake, watches Sir Joaquín Mendoza Peralejo run away, his brown loafers splashing through the farm road.

"What a funny fellow. Noy, what do you think of Sir Joaquín Mendoza Peralejo?"

Beroy mocks the Spanish intonation in which Sir Joaquín Mendoza Peralejo always said his name. Always with a Sir, and always his full name, as if convincing himself that his name was indeed his own.

Rising from the wet, muddy ashes of the carabao's back, Jojo watches Sir Joaquín Mendoza Peralejo's escape from what he must think is the sight of their savagery. This devastates her, and she believes Beroy had made her look as much a brute as Sir Joaquín Mendoza Peralejo most certainly assumed before delivering himself to their humble rural town.

"There's seriously something very wrong about the man" says Beroy as he examines the length of the small snake.

Jojo leans forward, and her carabaos shifts; the children both snap their ropes to keep their carabaos from moving about. "Hoooold. I said hold—why—hold. Hold! You Filthy Animal!" Her command pierces through Beroy's ear, while the carabaos look drunk with tension. Jojo glowers at Beroy, and commands him to give her the dead snake.

"I said let me see it! Give me my snake!"

"Hey now, why are you—" Beroy pauses before a realization dawns on him, "wait, what? Are you embarrassed about that? That guy?" he asks. "Really? *That* guy?" Beroy insists on highlighting the absurdity of the situation.

"No!" Jojo's denial is apparent. "Just give me the snake. It belongs to me!"

"Oh would you relax, Noy. *Calma lang bala.*"

"Calm for what? Sir Joaquín Mendoza Peralejo is elegant, and you should know your place in your future interactions with him. Now, snake. Give it to me."

Indignant, she stretches her hand and receives the snake. Beroy just watches her in amusement. Quietly this time so as not to rouse her inclination for vengeance since she is never forgiving when colored with ire.

Which is a strange thing, because she is a beautiful child. In Filipino conceptions of beauty, her lack of femininity always presents itself as a sharp juxtaposition because her masculine disposition rarely transcends the allure of her appearance. Society views her as traditionally beautiful with her pale white skin, and sleek black hair, yet in bouts of anger she embodies the temperance of a raging bull. Besides, Jojo also thinks being pretty is useless unless you want to work in a brothel for the rest of your life. A sentiment that she may have inherited from interactions with a father who bemoaned the reality of having a visually pleasing spouse. When men refer to her as a Geisha because of her porcelain skin, she responds with the invitation to arm wrestle her commentators. She only respects people who made the honor roll, and read in their free time. Someone like Sir Joaquín Mendoza Peralejo. He was rich—wealthy—and obviously despised himself for the source of his wealth, focusing instead on the value of his god-given intelligence, which made Jojo adore him even more.

Beroy never learned to read. And he thinks people like Sir Joaquín Mendoza Peralejo have no soul, bobbing about life, frantically trying to find themselves across oceans and continents without ever really finding happiness. Or love. Because they do the utter most, never finding a tribe because they would never learn to love themselves. Beroy feels sorry for him because he saw, in the eyes of Sir Joaquín Mendoza Peralejo, a tortured vacantness. He was a man who never loved himself enough to be truly happy because he lacked a critical gene for happiness: honesty. The entirety of his family line reeked of deceit and ill-gotten wealth. So long may he drown in the life of service to the people his family oppressed for three hundred years. These are insights you don't find in the pages of literature. So why read?

And before Beroy knows it, the snake lands—wet with mud—on his face. He understands this as Jojo's temper, manifested in a sweet, alluring charm that makes him smile more than it makes him angry. As Beroy washes the slime and mud off his face, Jojo has gotten off the carabao, and has decided to run away. She runs with zero regard for her dirty carabaos, and leaves Beroy with them.

He has the nerve to embarrass me, he should make himself useful then.

She finds a river closer to her family's mangrove to wash the slime and gunk off of her clothes. She is muttering to herself, completely consumed by anger at Beroy's audacity to laugh at her. From the poop on her *tsinelas*, to the snake in her hair, and the embarrassing encounter with her favorite teacher, she pushes her rage toward heaven, in full force, and howls for the Curse of Thunder in a prolonged, blood-curdling, "DeeeeeePoooooooTaaaaaaaaa!"

And so it rains.

She continues to stare upward, her mouth open in the melody of her anguish as raindrops plunge toward the tip of her tongue. However, the sun doesn't retreat behind the clouds. In a moment, the rain peters out, as if only passing by to rinse the slime of curses spewing off her bitter mouth. When the rain disappears completely, Jojo begins to cry in profound sorrow, frustrated by the series of unfortunate events that plagued her morning routine. Something softly flutters across her face, grazing the roundness of her cheeks.

She is calmed by the sight of a plane flying overhead across the rainbow. In pure amusement and wonder, she forgets her anguish and begins to wonder what it is like to ride an airplane.

When I become American, no one would ever laugh at me ever again.

She imagines a plane is like a house in the sky, full of beds and chocolates from all over the world. One time, Sir Joaquín Mendoza Peralejo bought her an airplane plush toy for her birthday. He said he won it in a mid-air trivia competition. Since then, she has always believed that airplanes must be a carnival ride full of games, food, and comfy beds for people to sleep in. She closes her eyes and finds herself inside the plane, winning the biggest teddy bear she has ever seen. One day, she will be aboard the skies, winning all the prizes of every trivia game played in flight.

As the world continues to turn, wiping away the grief and sadness on her face, a large brown butterfly lands on her yellow *tsinelas*. It lingers on her toes, and refuses to fly away as she blows in its direction. She fixes her gaze on the little brown creature and notices a faint shimmer of golden brown spattered across its back. She carefully lowers her finger, and the butterfly crawls off her *tsinelas* to hoist itself onto her fingers. Jojo's expression is dazed with wonder as she examines its beauty closely and says a soft "Wow…"

Startled, it flies away.

Voices of the Pacific Islands

Māmalahoa:
Law of the Splintered Paddle

Kirby Wright

Kirby Wright

Waves slam the sea cliffs of Puna. We are five war canoes, fighting through heavy waves. A *lei niho palaloa* hangs off my neck, its whale tooth suspended on a braid of human hair. My warriors wear gourd masks with *'uki* crests. My canoe is the red of the *'ohelo* berry. Lava pinnacles reach out, stabbing the ocean. The hands on our paddles are eager to plunder what belongs to the *ali'i*—the ruler of the district who destroyed our estates.

This edge of Hawai'i is ruled by Keawemauhili, the high chief I defeated at the Battle of Moku'ōhai. On that victorious day, I took the red feather cloak that once belonged to my cousin Kiwala'o. But time brings humility. I have learned a single victory does not make me *ali'i ai moku,* king of the islands. But the day will come when Puna belongs to me. One day, the Puna *maka'ainana*, the commoners, will call me king.

We paddle into Papa'i Bay. Green sand. Keiki fill *hala* baskets with seaweed—*limu*. The girls, *na wahine*, scoop *'opae* and pluck '*opihi* off oceanfront lava for food. I see the thatched walls of *hale noho*, a village behind a grove of *hau*—Hibiscus trees.

Who protects the people—these *maka'ainana*? Where are Puna's warriors? Keawemauhili pillaged Kohala and I will have revenge. We will slaughter all who challenge. My warriors will defile their *na wahine.*

We find passage through the reef. Girls fill floating calabashes roped to their waists. Men throw nets and spears. A conch shell in the village sounds—a danger warning. We reach the shallows. Will the villagers fight? Fight or not, we will take what we want. My red canoe slides over the sand and stops beside a *ku'ula*, a white coral altar. A *papio* offering bakes on stone. "*A'ole kanawai ma keia wahi,*" I tell my men, meaning there is no law in the village. They leap out knowing what happens here will be our secret. In Puna today, we will ravage.

Manō. We are hungry sharks hunting for blood. The na wahine run. The fishermen brandish short spears and knives meant for gutting *weke*. A stone off a *ma'a* sling flies past my face. A second *pohaku* strikes Kekuhaupi'o. I order the attack. Spears thrust hard into Puna flesh, and our *palua pu'ili*, double clubs, shatter bones. These Puna men have stone *poho,* and some swing *ko'oko'o* canes. Their weapons do little damage, but our sharp strikes wound and kill.

Na wahine flee for a distant coconut grove. My speedy men capture the girls and drag them into the *naupaka* shrubs. A fisherman tosses his net, entangling Kalena. This same man pulls a paddle from my canoe. He swings—the blade rips into Kalena's neck. I press the flaps of skin together to slow the bleeding. The fisherman lifts a small boy onto his shoulder and runs, holding the paddle. Kalena spits blood and dies.

I chase his killer, running with my *leiomano* over a lava ledge. I close in and am ready to strike, but my foot gets swallowed. I fall. *Auwe*—Dear God! My foot is caught in a fissure's mouth. The fisherman stops. He puts down the boy and grips the paddle's handle with both hands. He swings, and I arm-block the blow. His second swing is high, and the blade shatters against my head. Blood fills my eyes. He finds my leiomano, its shark teeth as white as bone. I tug at my foot. He raises the weapon, and I hear the calls of warriors. The fisherman hurls my leiomano into the sea, picks up the child and runs. My men reach me. Kekuhaupi'o lifts me, but my foot is caught. They want to chase down the fisherman. I tell them *no*.

Kekuhaupi'o spills *kukui* nut oil from a bowl down my leg. He grabs me at the armpits, twists my body, and lifts. Still trapped. He lifts again and the fissure releases my ankle. A girl applies seaweed and 'uki salve to my head and bandages me with *kapa* made from tree bark. *How can she care for me after the evil I have done?*

We return to our canoe and paddle for Kona. My head throbs. My heart breaks.

Who is Kamehameha? I am king of murderers, thieves, and rapists. We are plunderers. Pirates. A gang of killers attacking without warning, a tribe feasting on fear. *How is this fair?*

Hurting and killing innocents is not revenge against a rival king, but cruelty. There is no reward when a warrior kills a common man. There is only shame and grief. Killing without purpose will destroy our *mana*, our spiritual power. Should a rival king attack, we will fight. But we will no longer attack the innocent people living in his territory.

From this day forward, the maka'ainana will not suffer. They will not fear the attacks of those who are stronger. *Pele,* the fire goddess, swallowed my foot. I beg for forgiveness. No longer will villagers be attacked alongside any coast or in the uplands, or on any *ahupua'a,* where the land divides the mountain and sea.

I will take the lives of those who disobey.

A Dinner Engagement with Mister Top Hat

Douglas Perenara Johnston

Huia woke up with a reddish light coming through the window. The bruised sky was a mosaic of reds, apricots, oranges, and tangerines. She always liked to look at the sunrise with a sheet over her head, imagining it being akin to a mother's womb. Not a real birth, but the birth of a new day. A beautiful morning then, but as the saying goes, Red sky in the morning, shepherd's warning. Huia always saw it as a wise saying; a day usually started perfectly, and any disappointments came later.

She turned over in bed and saw that Mereaira was already up, her bed made with military precision, as always. Mereaira liked to set an example for her younger sister. Sighing, Huia sat up as Mereaira appeared in the doorway, taller at twelve years old to Huia's seven.

“Good, you're awake,” said Mereaira. “Hurry up, lazybones, Mama's got breakfast ready."

"Okay, I'll be there in a tick," replied Huia.

In the kitchen, Huia's senses were assaulted by a bevy of wonderful smells: freshly baked rewena bread, crispy bacon, poached eggs, fresh milk, and porridge. Mama was at the stove loading plates with kai as Huia's older brothers, Hemi and Arapeta, came into the kitchen.

“Good morning, Mama. Thank you,” said Huia, accepting a heaping plate and waiting for Mama to say grace.

Today was no different than any other day, so after breakfast, Huia and Mereaira would help their brothers milk the cows before school.

“Just a minute, kids,” Mama said. “I almost forgot to tell you before you run out the door. I want you girls to ask your teacher, Mister Potae, to dinner tonight. Your Nana mentioned that he is a relative from my side of the whanau and your uncle. It is important to keep whanau ties strong, aye, girls. We'll have your favourite roast beef with all the trimmings and rice pudding. Won't that be nice?"

“Ah, yes Mama,” Huia said, looking wide-eyed over at Mereaira on the way out the door.

Hemi snickered at her as they all ran over to milk the cows. "Oh no, you and Mereaira don't like Mister Potae, do you, Huia? Didn't he used to give you girls the strap?"

"Only because we were late to school because certain lazy louts ran off after milking, so we have to cart all the milk to the road ourselves," Mereaira retorted.

The boys just laughed and ran ahead.

"I just know they will do the same again this morning, too. Luckily, we have Dollar to ride to school now," Huia said.

Dollar had at first seemed an odd name for a horse to Huia, as they used pounds, shillings, and pence in New Zealand. She thought riding horses must make Mereaira think of the American wild west or something. Mereaira's face brightened at the mention of her beautiful horse. The girls now rode double to school and left the horse at an uncle's place who lived nearby. Mereaira's face darkened. Huia knew what she was thinking.

"I can't believe we have to ask Mister Top Hat to dinner, Huia," Mereaira fumed. "Do we have to? I don't want to, even if he is our uncle."

Mister Top Hat was their nickname for Mister Potae. Potae could mean hat in English. It was like one of their Tokona cousins who was called Suzy Socks because Tokona sounded like Tokena, which meant socks in English.

"I don't want to either, but what can we do?" Huia said. "Mama will be disappointed if we don't. Still, at least we'll have a great dinner… and Mama's rice pudding, too. I guess I could survive sitting near him if the kai is so good."

The girls had a good reason for not liking Mister Top Hat. When the children first started going to Matata Māori School, they would wait at the roadside for the bus that took them the three miles from the farm into the village. This all changed in 1952 when they pinched the bus off the kids for the workers at the new Tasman Mill in Kawerau.

After the kids lost their bus and before they had horses to ride to school, they had to walk the three miles. The roads were all gravel, and their shoes were not always of the best quality. Huia and Mereaira had often followed the railway track, holding hands, and walking one to a rail to avoid the rough ballast in between. Sometimes the train drivers would give them a ride since Pa worked on the railways.

With the girls having to carry the milk to the road, they were often late, and this was when Mister Top Hat would give them the strap. He never cared for any excuses and therefore the girls were faced with the dilemma of having to ask him to dinner without wanting him to accept.

"What should we do?" asked Mereaira, throwing a blanket over Dollar after they had finished taking the milk can to the roadside.

"We don't have any choice. We can't NOT ask him because Mama will find out… Now we know he is our uncle, too."

"She wouldn't give us a hiding or anything, Huia."

"Yes, but she will be disappointed in us. That's enough, Mereaira." Huia pointed out.

"Yeah, I guess you're right."

The girls schemed, even considering skipping school altogether - but came up with no way out of their dilemma. After leaving Dollar at Uncle's place, they walked through the memorial gateway at school. They paused to touch their Uncles' name on the World War Two pillar. Pa's two youngest brothers, Eru and Tama, had gone to war. One had not returned.

The school day began with the 9 am bell ring that signaled the children to line up for inspections. Everyone had their hands, hair and teeth checked to make sure they were clean. Next came the march around the sports field, then off to class. The school boasted four classrooms to house classes for the new entrants through to form two. A highlight of every day was the free milk for all children at morning break.

Huia and Mereaira approached Mister Top Hat grudgingly near home time. A tall man, he stood with his large muscular arms crossed over his barrel chest. His look was stern and forbidding, with frown lines prominent and thick eyebrows drawn down over deep-set dark eyes.

"Excuse me, Mister Potae, my mother asked us to invite you to dinner tonight as you are related to our whanau from Tauranga Moana," Huia said hesitantly.

"From Tauranga?" He asked, sounding surprised with widening eyes. "What is your mother's whanau name?"

"Tokona, sir," replied Huia.

"Ah, Tokona. Yes, we are whanau then, girls. That would make me your uncle. How wonderful," Mister Top Hat beamed, and his eyes softened. He looked friendly for the first time Huia could remember. She usually feared him. Now she had mixed feelings.

"Yes… uncle. We hope you can come," said Mereaira.

"Of course, I'd love to," he replied, sounding happy.

After school, Mereaira grew thoughtful and pointed out that although they had no choice in inviting him to dinner, the girls didn't need to turn up to dinner themselves - an intriguing idea.

"But then we will miss out on the roast, and the rice pudding," Huia argued. "He knows he is our uncle too. Now he'll probably treat us better."

"Ha, we're Māori sis. We call every adult in Matata uncle or aunty," Mereaira countered. "Anyway, let's swing by the Marae and see what's happening. I hear there is a bit of a hui going on."

The two girls ran up the hill to the Marae. Rangitihi was the name of the Marae, and the Wharenui was called Rangiaohia. The girls loved this place as all the buildings were named after their Tupuna, their kin. As they passed the Wharekai Rakauheketara, the girls were called over by their Aunty Ripeka, who was cutting up kumara and potatoes for the hangi. She saw the gloomy look on the girls' faces and asked what was wrong.

"We had to ask our teacher, Mister T…, I mean Mister Potae, to dinner because Mama said he was our uncle," Huia admitted.

"Ah, Mister Potae, he IS your uncle. What's the problem, girls?" Aunty Ripeka asked.

"He used to strap us for being late when we had to milk the cows before going to school, so we don't want to be there," Mereaira explained.

"Did he now?" Aunty Ripeka said dangerously. "Don't go then."

"Excuse me?" Huia said.

"Don't go. Stay here and have a kai with us, sweetie."

Mereaira and Huia grinned at each other.

"Mama would probably be disappointed if we didn't come to dinner. Mum made rice pudding too," Mereaira protested weakly.

"I'll ring your mama and tell her we needed you to help with the chores in the Wharekai. I guess you will just have to survive on boring old hangi pork, chicken, duck, and steamed pudding. There is also boil up with brisket, doughboys, and watercress… I think someone made a pav and there may even be some rice pudding," Aunty Ripeka said with a wink.

"Duty calls, sis," Huia said to Mereaira with a grin.

"Yes, I guess we'll miss our dinner engagement with Mister Top Hat," Mereaira replied with a giggle.

"What a shame, all right," Huia agreed with delight.

"Everything is in hand, for now, girls, so go and enjoy yourselves. Later I'll be having words with your teacher about the strappings. So, not to worry, it will never happen again," Aunty Ripeka said, with a steely look in her eye.

"Thank you, Aunty, you're the best," Mereaira said.

"We can go and pay our respects in the urupa to our Tupuna then we can go play with the other kids before the kai is ready," Huia suggested.

"Good idea, let's go," said Mereaira, racing Huia to the urupa.

"At least YOUR uncle should be nicer to us now," Huia teased.

"YOUR uncle," Mereaira countered.

"YOUR uncle," Huia laughed.

After their visit to the urupa, Huia had a frown on her face as she thought about tonight's dinner.

"What's up sis?" Mereaira asked.

"We need to go home." Huia said simply.

"But Aunty Ripeka has organized everything. We're in the clear," Mereaira objected, happy with the arrangement of staying at the Marae.

"I don't want to disappoint Mama. She is going to a lot of effort over dinner. Things will be better now that Mr. Potae knows we're family… I hope." Huia was determined now.

Mereaira finally agreed, "I supposed you're right," but sighed in regret over missing the feast at the Marae.

They informed Aunty Ripeka, who understood. She did still ring mama and tell her about the strapping the girls received from Mr. Potae, though. Mama outdid herself with dinner. Everything was delicious and everyone enjoyed themselves. Mr. and Mrs. Potae got on well with Mama and Papa. The children found their aunty and uncle to be quite friendly – Huia and Mereaira hoped this would last with their uncle. They found their aunty to be lovely. One awkward moment came during dessert when Mama brought up the girls being strapped. She mentioned that Aunty Ripeka had informed her after being confided in by the girls. The girls then explained why they had been late, and their uncle apologized and promised it would never happen again. It turned out that Hemi and Arapeta were the ones to get in trouble with Papa for leaving the girls to carry to milk to the road. In the end, Huia and Mereaira were glad to attend the dinner.

Ram Raid

Douglas Perenara Johnston

Golden Peaks Station was a large high-country farm with an enviable reputation. Golden Peaks also ran a small award-winning vineyard and cellar door with a busy restaurant selling their own craft beers, olive oil, manuka honey, and sheep and goats' cheese. The Paterson family, owners for seven generations, were prominent in the district and active in the community. But it was another who proved to be the genuine character of the station and the surrounding district. He wasn't a Paterson; he wasn't even human. His name was Casanova, and his name and legend would soon spread throughout the land. This is his story.

Casanova the ram had already secured himself an infamous reputation at Golden Peaks. This in some part contributed to his name, as he was not named because of his love life… though he was a fine breeder (a fact that saved him from the chopping block). No, Snow Paterson dubbed the cantankerous ram Casanova because of the beast's penchant for charging people when they weren't looking and literally "sweeping them off their feet."

Snow loved Casanova, probably because the touchy beast reminded him of his own sunny disposition (not). He also valued him because of his strong breeding performance. Moth also took a liking to the recalcitrant ram, for this reason, as the station produced some of the finest stock in the country, largely because of Casanova. There was also the fact that the ram seemed to have an instinctive understanding with the two big men not to push his luck with them.

Casanova also didn't mess with the Māori shearers who came every season. They teased him, but also gave him treats. Perhaps he took their threats of being part of the boil up or hangi seriously? Still, things seemed to have calmed down at Golden Peaks, and with workers being more aware. They made sure there were no bright colours, sudden loud noises, or shining lights to startle Casanova. All seemed well.

Bryn Paterson, or Moth to his friends, ran the station with his father Snow.. Moth liked to think he received the moniker because he worked until after dark. The real reason was, if there was a party, and there were lights on, he'd be drawn in, no fail… much to the lament of his wife.

Snow's sobriquet would seem obvious with his great shock of white hair and beard, but again, there was another explanation. Snow had always been a handsome man, with a dynamism that drew people to him. But like actual snow, he was "pretty" to view from a distance, but not nearly so pleasant up close. Casanova matched the men in personality, so they got on.

One evening, as the setting sun set a fiery halo over the heads of the rapidly darkening peaks, Casanova turned his head and slowly surveyed his domain. This season had been fruitful. His ewes had produced ample numbers of his progeny, his bloodline assured. Even the cattle knew not to challenge him. Reminiscing was not usually in Casanova's nature, so he moved on from his musing and quickly noted that not all was as it should be in his kingdom.

The paddock next to him held some of his most precious breeding ewes or was meant to. Seeing no other recourse, Casanova simply went to the place in the fence where he could get through and quickened his pace, as the paddock indeed proved empty. As he reached the other side, Casanova found a gate open, and his girls had escaped! The ram followed the trail left by his ewes as quickly as he dared in the failing light until he suddenly pulled up short. Casanova raised his large shaggy head in dismay and looked down a long slope towards the bright lights and loud noises of "town." This mythical place where humans gathered like… well, cattle to make… *NOISE*, *bright lights*, and be *colourful,* all the things he hated. He turned and looked back to discover with a shock how far from his domain he had come.

Casanova took stock but decided he couldn't let his girls down. He followed them off the hills into the bright lights of what to humans was a small to middling tourist oasis. To the ovine species, this was another universe of terrors, wonders, and perhaps delights. As he made his way through the streets, he soon spotted some of his girls and called out to them.

"Baaaa!"

His commanding presence and familiar tone brought them running, as many were not so taken with the delights that their first trip to town offered. Luckily, most of the ewes had not been as bold as Casanova and were slower to explore. He made rapid progress in tracking down his wayward flock in anticipation of returning to greener pastures. As it was a weeknight, the town seemed relatively quiet… so far, so good.

Casanova was strolling past a large store when he glanced sideways into the glass doors of the front entrance. The moon, a beautiful full one the colour of a ripe nectarine, came out from behind the clouds. The light highlighted Casanova's reflection in all his majestic glory. Casanova was an impressive-looking ram, large, powerful, and intimidating. Unfortunately, he didn't understand that he was looking at a reflection of himself. All he knew was a serious rival stood there calmly eyeballing him arrogantly. The nerve! There was no backing down from this rascal… in front of his girls on unfamiliar turf as well. He could lose everything. He backed off and went through his famed pre-charge ritual, sparing not a grunt nor a scowl, and scraped at the strange grey surface of the street. The other ram before him was deliberately copying his every move, as if to taunt him! You dare? Eyes flat now, Casanova dropped his head and charged. CRASH! The sound of shattering glass broke the relative quiet of the night and sent the assembled ewes scampering in all directions.

Casanova came to a screeching halt in shock, largely because he didn't feel the heavy blow he expected, the heavy strike to his rival that he NEEDED to feel. Instead, what seemed like thousands of little sleet or hailstones struck him, cutting him, and no enemy was to be found. He bolted in panic a short distance, but soon returned, determined to investigate further. He decided enemies didn't just disappear and then heard noises from further on in the dark shop. Something was in there and Casanova was going to find out what.

At the same time Casanova was charging his reflection at the main entrance, youths thought it would be a brilliant idea to use a stolen car to ram through the side entrance. They planned to help themselves to the latest and coolest free clothing and accessories. Then they'd get out quick, split the ill-gotten gains, torch the car, and go their separate ways. Genius. One thing they had not accounted for, though, on their first ram-raid was coming face to face with a very real and very annoyed ram.

Our young miscreants had targeted a large SUV rented out to foreign tourists whose English wasn't so great. They reasoned that this would delay any stolen vehicle reports and provide ample room for plunder. They were all kitted out with gloves and balaclavas, so any CCTV footage wouldn't incriminate them. One of them, who fancied himself the "criminal mastermind," a skinny redhead kid with freckles called Glynn, even came up with a novel way to ensure they did not spend too long in the shop, lowering chances of being caught. He put a ripped CD in the car with only one song on it, the 1978 classic Split Enz classic *I See Red*, off the CD he'd pinched off his douche of an uncle.

The plan was to hit play as soon as they breached the shop and do the raid. They would be back in the car and on their way by the time the song's three minutes and fifteen seconds were up. He'd also got everyone to set the stopwatch on their smartphones and they had done a dry run to time things just out of town. The old fogie song choice had caused groans among the teens, but it added to the fun and highlighted the age gap between them and adults.

"Even if we got caught, we're only kids. What can they do? They can't touch us. Suckers," Glynn had gloated.

Casanova's bad mood increased as loud music and singing battered his ears. He ran through the front part of the shop and collided with Declan – both stopped, startled. Declan made the mistake of thinking Casanova was a harmless sheep and excitedly pulled out a can of red spray paint. He proceeded to spray a generous streak down Casanova's flank.

"I see red," the song belted out in the background.

"There's a live bloody sheep in here, ha-ha. You said not to tag the shop, but I tagged him instead. Look!" Declan turned to his cohorts and pointed back proudly. Big mistake.

"I see red," the song repeated.

Casanova sized up the youth with back turned nicely towards him. He lowered his head and charged, sending the fool into a large glass thing another human was attacking with a fake leg.

"Declan's been taken out by a sheep!" Screamed Tyrone, trying to pick up Gordy, who was flailing on the floor with a mannequin's leg.

Every eye in the room turned to Casanova, and then all hell broke loose. Teenage boys panicked, yelling, and running in all directions as Casanova went on the rampage.

Cue rapid piano solo in the song as…

Casanova easily caught another victim as he stood frozen in place.

"Mama, Mama, help me!" cried Tyrone before he was rundown, even as the ram lost his footing and skidded around corners on the shiny shop floors. To add insult to injury, the clop, clop, clop sound of Casanova's cloven hooves gaining on him upset Tyrone so much that he ended up… ahem, soiling himself.

By the time the piano solo concluded, three of the five youths were down, with 2: 52 up on the track.

Into the intense guitar solo…

Casanova next downed a youth attempting to seek refuge in the stolen car. He was knocked out against the side of it. The impact, and the youth's demise, was perfectly in time with the music…

"Hey!" Went the song.

Outside the shop, the nervous ewes had returned to witness the final comeuppance as Glynn, crouching and crying, was repeatedly battered against the window of the shop.

"I see red, I see red, I see red, I see red"

"I see red, I see red, I see red, I see red"

"I see red, I see red, I see red, I see red" 3:15, end of song.

Casanova made his way out of the shop, exhausted, and found his ewes waiting for him. He had had enough of town, he decided, with its bright lights, noises, and strangeness. It was time to go back to where he belonged, so he headed off before they ran into any more humans. Thankfully, he didn't glance in any more shop windows to see another brazen challenger. Especially one sporting bright red paint this time, or God knows what would have happened.

A day or two passed at Golden Peaks Station and the flock had fallen back into their natural rhythm. Casanova was back in his rightful position as Lord of own little Realm. All was as it should be, except the sticky substance applied to his side and the farm staff's curiosity as to its source. Snow, being his usual charming self, had nearly caused a feud with one of the neighbouring farms by accusing them of attacking his prized Ram out of jealousy.

The truth eventually came out when CCTV of the ram-raid made the news. Casanova was instantly recognisable. The paint now made total sense. The prize-winning Ram became an internet sensation overnight. Some news reporters from the Big Smoke even came out to Golden Peaks to "interview" the new star and his owners. Considering they turned up in a helicopter, their reception on arrival was not as pleasant as they imagined. To sum it up, the TV3 reporter picked the WRONG day to wear a pink shirt and expensive shoes. Casanova's fame only seemed to grow.

The town held a reception for the ram in town as a guest of the mayor. The day was bright with an almost carnival atmosphere. Such was his fame that visitor numbers to town had increased. They had given a colossal statue of the famous ram pride of place downtown. So they took Casanova down to the town he thought he'd never need to see again. He gazed up at the statue they erected of him, red paint, and all…

"I see red."

He then gazed at all the people who came to see him and his magnificence. There was a festive feeling with lots of talking and laughing…

Noise...

He saw lots of cameras pointed at him, eager for a picture, flash, flash, flash.

Bright lights...

And then the mayor himself got up to speak through a loud PA system that distorted badly. He was a large man with a black robe and a huge shiny gold chain of office around his neck. The mayor had his hands crossed behind his backside, where he held a red A4-sized diary…

"I see red."

Snow and Moth looked at each other from their seats behind the mayor and rolled their eyes. The old gasbag could talk the door off a barn. Snow smiled and looked back at his prized ram, and the smile slipped from his face.

"My giddy aunt," Snow managed.

"Jesus wept," Moth blurted out, though it was unclear why he quoted John 11:35. It was impressive he knew an entire verse from the Bible by heart, not being a devout man, even if it was the shortest.

Casanova had escaped his rope, had fixated on the mayor's red diary, and readied himself, preparing to charge.

Voices of the Americas

Lincoyer

D.W. Simerly

—November 3, 1813.

The dark midnight-morning was a dark blanket over the Coosa River. A cool front, sopped with dew and carried by a lazy wind's breeze over the tepid green tumult. The near-daybreak air ached in a longing silence for the truncated calls of warbling songbirds—some subdued to stuttered utterances, some swelling to sleepy traces and melodic sweeps. Dense brush traced their leafed fingers on the slow rush of the water, and stray blades of supple grass lost their root, catching a ride into the running water. The water's movement was formed in the spaces across the rocks. Sheets of descending steps suggested slight falls of water, and zigzagging divots were encouraged by the sparse and jagged rocks.

In a hut, warmed by the sleepy drones of others, a mother lay with her baby clinging to her chest. The bundled armful was no less than ten moons old, and—despite his long, restful sleep—the mother had been awake, wide-eyed, listening to the wind. Her thoughts clawed their way through every snapping branch, every sepulchral sigh. She lay there all night, waiting to hear their grating language and the flapping of their blue-cloth coats in the wind, but the call to night was fierce, and she dozed off—her breaths heaving along with her son. The boy's father once sang to warm her. She thought about a scullery fire splitting the air; it softened and warmed her ears just enough to let her sleep.

She dreamed 19 moons ago, coiled with her lover by the riverbed, shaded by the high flanking leaves of a cedar tree. They were a world away, growing a garden together, and after they finished planting, a hearty wind swept through the branches, their limbs swaying.

The mother went back the next day and chewed the leaves they'd sown. Her belly swelled with the moons. He'd paint the clouds' moon gown with smoke from the leaves.

Her sleep was a long blink—short and lonely. She woke up to the boy's crying and the boisterous sounds of rifles breaking the air. She ran to the hut entrance, welcomed by blood-gargling screams. His red club—normally propped close to the entrance—was gone, as was he. The air was smoldering with burning wood and grass and meat—human tallow. She coughed at the density of the fog, then puked when the waft of burning flesh flooded her nostrils. She spat the residual bile that lingered and stood back upright, the baby's cry still ringing in her ears. She wiped his running nose, then tried to shield the baby's face from the smoke. She ran toward another hut, her left foot slopping into a puddle, kicking up a mixture of rain and blood— seemingly purple in dew-light. She dodged bodies in the field. Some in blue, some not. She stepped on one. It made no sound.

She entered one of the homes. It was brimming with murmurs and wails of worry. Most of them were women and children; there was one male warrior, trying to calm everyone down. The mother read worry on the warrior's face, and his words gushed with false confidence as he reassured all of them of their safety, his voice quivering like the slush of the river foam.

The warrior pulled her aside to a dark corner of the hut, and whispered, "They are burning huts; they will make it here eventually." If she wanted herself and the boy to make it, they needed to run. "If you make it to the creek bed, you can hide and wait it out." The soldiers would eventually leave the area.

"That boy will be important," were his final words. There was no time to ask him questions.

She ran out of the hut, weaving blindly through the plumes of pyre smoke. She felt the way with the bottom of her feet; she knew the contours of the soil well, like the plumed cheeks on her baby's face, and his dense, dark eyebrows like little caterpillars.

She turned when her heel thumped on the cedar root and anticipated a decline in terrain and—finally—felt a dry, sparse greenery beneath her feet. Then the florid fog and smoke dispersed, and they were hidden away.

She was stuck—frozen for a second. She felt a tinge of pain in her back. A bayonet. She looked down and saw how the blade was rising from her chest. The soldier pulled out the bayonet, and she fell hard to the ground on her back. The baby did not cry. His head tucked to her, hidden in the curve of her body.

As the sun arched its way towards the high clouds, the baby's cries echoed across the rolling river. A pale-faced soldier grabbed the baby from the cold mother and walked him back to camp. He offered the boy to a pair of Mvskoke women held captive, their wrists bound in sweltering rawhide. They looked at the boy and the soldier and screamed with a vitriol that the soldier couldn't understand.

A fellow soldier intervened, claiming to know their tongue. "The baby's mother, family, and friends are dead," he said. "Just kill him."

The soldier was befuddled, and he shook his head as he ran towards the general's tent, baby in tow. The women watched in confusion as he ran away with the baby. One took a step towards him but was stayed by the other's hand. They cried together, humming, chanting into each other's ears through all that was and all that would come to pass: *Pum vpvltake vpēyvnna, mvn tehecvkvrēs.*

A Nationless People

Alysha Brooks

The Native "American" 1884-2025

They say my people are blood.
We are tally stains in red
a pie chart of personhood,
is all we are in the end.

They say my people are blood.
The spirits in red,
who dance in footsteps,
where blood they have shed.

They say my people are blood.
The same shade of their skin,
but yet, its mystery,
for the redskin is dead.

They say our blood was our right,
but there is no freedom,
unless the colour is white.
It is the American birthright.

The Native Myth

We are a myth,
a distant memory,
the one where you can't quite tell
if it was real or a dream.

We are a fairytale,
some sort of story of old,
lost in translation.
What was the moral once told?
A story passed down
from an amorphous face,
whose name somehow
you now can't quite seem to place.

We are a song,
no one quite knows the name.
Just some sort of feeling
of a time and a place.
A melody is there,
but the notes are all wrong,
and the words are unfocused,
no one sings along.
But the forest of course,
the wind, and the waves.

The spirits,
whose memory doth save.
Sing lively, and bright,
know each story by name.
Who remind us that we
are not but a myth
left to wither and waste.

Alysha Brooks

The Familiar Feeling of Doom

I'm glad they are dead.
My grandfather and
my grandmother too.
For they have seen terror,
they know what is true.

They know who were murdered,
they know who survived
and if they lived,
they would see that more will die.

For where will they go?
Once they've carded them away,
illegals immigrate
to a country
that was taken away.
They are right, it is not ours,
since they snatched it away.

So, where will they go?
I think to the grave.
Like they did long ago—
they will do it again.

They never did stop,
it is all the same
the perpetual bringing
of tournament and pain.

The familiar feeling,
the cycle replayed.
The killings became quiet,
a secret affair.
But now it will be in the open,
there's a putrescent note in the air.

I'm glad my grandfather is dead,
my grandmother too.
They could die with hope,
without the stench and the fumes
of histories re-exhumed.

The White Native

I am a reminder,
a white scar of the flesh.
The mark of a traitor,
white privilege coalesces,
a treason for safety
is the mark of the flesh.

Forever the reminder
of what once commenced
of rape,
of murder,
a mother's crying child,
of prison,
of plague,
of poverty,
of torture and trial.

That is the colour,
the mark of my skin.
They look at me
as a leper,
the colonial contagion within.

Off The Rez

They tell me not to go home
It wasn't really a home anyways—
a home of prescription
of hiding away.

I'm suppose be free,
I can go where I please,
except for my home
which is not home for me.

They were all rounded up
sometime ago
and told to stay
at the island of rose.

16 hours away,
but my father says not to go.
You're too white there—to stay
at the island of rose.
Even dead,
your grandfather didn't want to go
back 16 hours away
to the Island of Rose.

He left there,
not by choice,
but still all the same.
He left them,
and made his own way.

From the Island of Rose,
from the place
that was once his home.
Now you're left
16 hours away,
with no clan
and no name.

No way
to know
what the ancestors know,
and why should you?
Who gave you the right?
To know
what they know
on the island of rose?
You don't have to hold
all the pain that they hold.

The rez is not safe,
so my father has told,
especially for girls
who never lived
on the Island of Rose.

Howl at the Moon

Jordan Maison

When the Moon vanished from the sky there was a gathering. An unheard of gathering for unheard of times. Nations the world over traveled the wind and seas, guided to a singular place—which only the Greater Spirits could lay claim to. Rivalries, some of which spanned millenia, were set aside to address the greater concern.

The ancestors spoke of an ancient horror, the *manahas*, who preyed on the flesh of men. Too weak to stand against the light of the Sun, they used the night to carry out their transgressions. For centuries they terrorized the realms until Muhe took her place in the night sky as the Moon.

In the days following the Moon's disappearance, these ravenous creatures of darkness reclaimed the night. Bodies began to pile up—or would have if manahas left any scrap behind. Blessedly, the place they'd been led to, which sat somewhere between the Earth and Sky worlds, provided respite from the beasts.

Centered among the vast plains where the assembled nations camped sat a small, rather unassuming tent. Within the stretched hide, however, all the leaders of the world alongside their attendants, generals, and trusted elders amassed. Somehow, there was more than enough room to spread out. Campfires dotted the sea of people like stars in the sky.

The space was filled with a hushed cacophony of whispers. Everyone talking, sharing their fears, yet unwilling to give them any volume even in this safe place. With so much going on, it was easy to overlook the lone child hiding near the back, watching intently.

Of course this meeting was no place for a mere child, but children are often driven by curiosity more than sense. Thus, Ahmik was able to witness a wondrous sight as the Greater Spirits arrived to commune with their children.

One moment the raised dais in the center was empty, and the next it was filled with a radiant light so strong it hurt the eyes to look upon. And yet, none were able to look away.

Ahmik watched, rapt, as the light faded into six distinct shapes. Most took on the form of people, chiseled warriors all, while a couple donned their animal shapes. Ahmik felt no fear upon seeing the giant Bear and Spider, for these were often the first Spirits children were taught.

He felt warmth on his cheeks and realized tears were streaming down his face. He took a moment to wipe the tears, but upon re-opening his eyes, the Spirits had shifted into new forms. Where bronze skin was once visible, darker shades and pale silver now shown through. Bear's black fur had turned golden brown, while Spider's once spindly legs were now thick and tufted with fur. Another blink and they'd changed again; a constant transformation reflecting the people of the world.

The Spirits arrayed themselves in a circle, in the middle of which a light continued to shine brightly. It too began to take on a different shape, though it was neither man nor beast. It seemed to be all at once; a being made of light itself. Naku, the Sun.

Naku scanned the gathered nations, his gaze spreading warmth everywhere he looked. For the first time since the Moon had vanished, Ahmik felt fear release its icy grip on his heart.

"My children," Naku's voice filled the cavernous tent. Despite keeping his voice low and measured, it nonetheless reached everyone's ears clearly.

"Our enemy has struck, and Muhe—" Naku faltered. It was the briefest of moments, a hitch in his throat, but revealed an all too human emotion: pain. The story of Sun and Moon's love was a tale for the ages, so the sorrow was to be expected. Seeing that pain laid bare, however, sucked the warmth from the room. A chilling reminder of the threat that remained.

"Muhe, has been taken," Naku finished, collected once more.

A tumult of voices with endless questions flooded the tent. Naku allowed it to continue for a moment before raising his hand (claw? wing?), instantly bringing silence. "Do not concern yourselves with how it happened. The manaha have been fighting us since before the dust was born on this world. Just know we've ensured their little *trick* will not be possible again."

"Great Naku," a leader called out. In the air above the Spirits, a shimmering image of the speaker appeared so that all could listen clearly.

"What can we do? These creatures know no fear. Our blades and arrows pass through them like swirling mist. This darkness is making our animals restless, souring them. Even the wolves have grown bolder."

"That, child, is why we are here now," Naku answered as the speaker's image faded away. "On top of being our friend, Muhe served an important purpose."

A new image shimmered in the air above the Spirits, showing a terrible sight: a manaha. Wispy and wraithlike, it held no specific form; a grotesque shadow with claws and a tooth-filled maw that never quite closed.

Ahmik shuddered and for the first time began to regret his decision to intrude on this conclave. He watched the vision-manaha as it slithered through the air until a moonbeam sliced into its path. It hissed as its skin sizzled in the silvery light and flitted away.

"Without Muhe's light," Naku continued over the fading imagery, "there is little to keep the manaha at bay in your world. It is a task we cannot leave vacant for long."

"Why can't we stay here?" A chieftain called out. "For the first time in days, our people have been able to rest easy, without fear. Can we not stay on this land?"

A murmur of voices rose in agreement, carrying on before Naku spoke over the tumult, "Our worlds are not meant to cross. This is a transitory place. What you grow—what you need—to live and thrive will not take root here.

"The longer we spend in this between-place, the weaker our protection becomes. Eventually, the manaha *will* find a way inside. If that comes to pass, they'll have the key to all worlds…"

Silence fell upon the crowd as the import of Naku's words sunk in. Manaha in their world was terrifying, but an invasion of the Sky Realm would be the end of all things forever.

"There is another option," a new voice chimed in with a grandmotherly timbre; the Spider. "We seek a replacement for Muhe. A new moon to fill the sky and serve as guardian."

"We will continue our work to free Muhe," Naku interjected quickly. "We will *not* abandon the Great Mother…But the world cannot wait for us to succeed."

The air thrummed with the weight of thousands of voices. Each clamoring to volunteer; all eager to serve even knowing it would mean separation from family and loved ones.

"I'm heartened to see such devotion," Naku spoke softly, forcing those gathered to quiet in order to hear. "The honor I see among you is boundless. I expected no less, but…"

The Greater Spirit paused and Ahmik felt himself holding his breath. "...But," Naku continued, "Whoever volunteers must be a child. No more than thirteen Summers."

The gathering erupted. Elders cried out, demanding an explanation, beating their breasts in frustration. Others wailed at the implication. As the stories told, there was no back and forth between realms. One had to leave their body behind in order to make the crossing.

The assembled spirits remained silent; letting the uproar continue unabated. This was a grief that could not be rushed.

Ahmik watched as a semblance of calm eventually rolled over the people. Hush fell as groups sat back down around their fires, an unmistakable weariness to their movements and far off gazes. Though his young mind could not understand the reason for it, Ahmik knew mourning when he saw it. These were the same looks he remembered on people's when his parents had died protecting the village.

"We know what it is we ask, but there is no other way." Naku spoke calmly. "The mind of a child is more…open, where an older person's mind is set; rigid in how it views the world. The things you would see, the task you must undertake, would drive anyone older mad. A potential eternity of torment for the volunteer, and an ineffective guardian for everyone else.

"Go now," Naku spoke louder, the voice of command. "You have some time before we must move from this between-place. Not much, but enough to discuss and make your—"

"I'll go!" The words were out of Ahmik's mouth before he fully registered he was talking. In a blink, the boy found himself directly in front of the Greater Spirits and feeling the heat radiating off Naku's (suddenly large) form. From hiding in the shadows of the strange tent, Ahmik now commanded the attention of all those gathered. He should have been terrified, and yet all he felt was calm.

"I'll go," Ahmik repeated. "I will fill in for Muhe."

A murmur rushed through the tent, along with the occasional call for him to sit back down. Ahmik ignored it all. He had eyes only for Naku as the Greater Spirit "kneeled" down. Ahmik was shocked to find eyes staring back at him, kindly despite the swirling flames within them.

Warm hands (or what felt like hands) cradled his face as Naku spoke softly, "My child. You have *heard*, but are you sure you know what it is we ask?"

A rush of heat filled Ahmik's cheeks. Of course Naku had known he was hiding the whole time and listening in. "I know," Ahmik answered.

"You know your stories?"

"Yes."

"You know it can be a lonely task? That we must always stay apart, never to interact but once a year?"

Ahmik nodded. The story of Naku and Muhe's love was also one of sacrifice. A price to be paid for the world, and children, they'd created. A story Ahmik had heard recounted for as long as he could remember. Still, he didn't waver. Putting himself forward had felt right. In some ways, it felt like there was no choice at all to be made.

"My parents died protecting me," Ahmik's voice was firm. "Can I do no less than live to protect others?"

Ahmik sensed, rather than saw, Naku's smile as the Great Spirit returned to his full height. "The decision is made," he called out, once more addressing the crowd. "Return to your people and tell them of Ahmik's bravery. Tell them a new guardian rises in the sky tomorrow."

As the elders, and the entourages, began filing out of the tent as they were bade, Ahmik quietly asked, "Will I be ready by tomorrow?"

Naku placed a warm, comforting, arm upon Ahmik's shoulder, "Dear child, you already have everything you need."

In the days that followed, Ahmik experienced wonders beyond description and settled into his new role—life—rapidly. He'd sunk easily into the rhythm of his nightly journey across the sky and his glowing light brought peace back to the land.

The manaha had been banished to the shadows and a general sense of normalcy returned. As the days turned into weeks, the youth which had made him ideal for the task also made him restless. He wanted to be more than a passive protector.

Ahmik had learned quickly the manahas weren't the only things stalking the night with foul intentions. Too often the evils he found happening in the dead of night were done by those of his own people. Assaults, thievery, and far more shocking things were taking place.

With the manaha threat no longer imminent, Ahmik turned his attention to these other, "lesser" evils. Shining upon their deeds wouldn't sizzle their skin and send them fleeing as it did with the manaha, but he had found his voice. Much like Naku and his spirit brethren demonstrated in the tent, Ahmik found he could communicate with a great number of people all at once.

From there, it was a simple matter of alerting the appropriate village elders, or others nearby who could intercede. From cities to villages, and even the wandering peoples of the plains, he used his newfound abilities to bring the wicked into a different kind of light.

Ahmik felt great joy in his sense of purpose; in helping those who would otherwise go unnoticed in the night. His luminance exposed those who would bring ruin to all people. What could be more incredible than that?

And yet…

Ahmik's moonlight could not fill all the dark spaces. There were still dreadful voids his light couldn't reach. Places in which evil lurked and schemed. It was here a group of men met and considered the unthinkable: conspiring with monsters.

In the bramble wikiup they'd built deep in the forest over the course of weeks, a handful of men hunched around a fledgling fire under the thatched dome. They waited long into the night, until Ahmik's moon had passed into a different part of the world. When their fire was little more than glowing embers, casting harsh shadows upon their hard faces, they whistled as one.

Four sharp, quick whistles echoed into the night and the forest grew eerily still. Even the rustling of bugs in the underbrush ceased, blanketing the area in an unnatural silence.

"You risk summoning us," a low voice hissed, breaking the quiet and jolting the men. They shrank deeper into the wikiup, inching closer together despite knowing there would be no safety in greater numbers.

Somehow, the space inside the hut grew even darker as the men sensed, rather than saw, the manaha as it filled the entrance. "You wanted our attention," it growled. "You have it. Now speak, say what you will before we feast."

The men exchanged furtive glances before one gathered enough courage to speak. "We must get Muhe back in the sky," he whispered.

The manaha laughed; a terrible, mirthless sound that sent chills down the men's spines. Without warning, a tendril of darkness lashed forward over the dwindling campfire. The man who'd spoken clasped his neck, struggling to stem the flow of blood now pouring from between his fingers. As the manaha's laughter at last subsided, their fellow conspirator slumped over, lifeless.

"Your opportunities to speak grows shorter," it snarled.

"Hear us, please!" Another man cried. "What we seek will also aid you!"

A heavy silence fell upon the cramped wikiup. At last, the creature spoke, "Continue."

"The boy-moon plagues us as well," the man continued, rushing the words out as quickly as possible. "His gaze threatens to expose us, leaving us cast out. With Muhe's return, he would be forced out."

"And this helps *us* how?" The manaha asked. With another flick of its talons, the number of conspirators dwindled by one more. "Her light, the boy's light. It makes no difference to us who occupies the sky."

"Y—you have Muhe, but can—cannot touch her," one of the remaining men stammered. "But we can. We can cover her with clay and mud. We can make her light dimmer before she ascends, allowing you more freedom to explore the night."

The manaha sat motionless, stirring only slightly as it leaned forward, "And what of the other spirits? Surely they would not suffer such a thing lightly."

"We make the switch at dusk, just as Ahmik begins his journey. We'll offer him a new shape in our world and by the time the switch is uncovered, it will be too late for the Great Spirits to do anything." The man ceased talking, shrinking against the side of the wikiup, hoping his words would prove sufficient for the manaha.

A soft click-click sound bounced around the enclosed space as the creature tapped its spindly claw against one of its longer teeth. The men exchanged nervous glances, pointedly ignoring the cooling bodies of their two fellow conspirators. They waited for the manaha to decide.

The clicking sound abruptly stopped. "Two nights," it said decisively. "Be here and we will show you to Muhe."

Collectively, the men sighed but the manaha cut their relief short, "Know this! Betray us, and no amount of light will spare you your fates."

Wordlessly, they nodded and in the next instant the dark creature was gone along with the two bodies. The deal struck, the men fled into the night, racing home to wait and prepare.

Ahmik beamed as he prepared to set about his nightly travels. Each evening brought a different slice of the world under his sight and more troublemakers to expose. It was tiring work, but he started each vigil fresh and eager.

As he was about to set out, however, a strange thing happened. He heard voices calling out to him. Over the months, Ahmik had grown accustomed to others offering praise and cheers directly to him, but this was different. Something more urgent.

Though the sky beckoned, Ahmik cast his gaze downward and saw a trio of men flailing their arms, shouting for his attention. "Great Ahmik-moon!" They called. He pulled himself closer and the light emanating from his body caused the three men to shield their eyes.

"We bring good news! Muhe has been found and freed."

"Truly?" Ahmik asked.

"Gaze upward and see for yourself," the men implored.

Ahmik shifted his attention skyward and gasped. There he spotted the Mother-moon, taking her place among the heavens exactly as he'd been preparing to do.

She looked…different from what he remembered. Her light was weaker, absent in some places, as dark spots dotted her once flawless skin along with a host of scuffs and bruises. It called to mind a memory Ahmik had of playing with other kids; tumbling roughly in the dirt. These weren't the marks from playful moments, however, but the result of whatever she'd endured in captivity.

The realization brought great anger to Ahmik's heart. Perhaps sensing his attention, Muhe looked down and caught Ahmik's eye. With a quick nod and small smile, the fury welling within Ahmik faded into joy at seeing her rise once more.

"Come, come," the men called, pulling Ahmik's awareness back down. "You must come with us. There cannot be two moons in the sky!"

Ahmik knew they were right, but felt reluctant to leave. "Where am I to go now?" He inquired.

"We've been sent to give you your new task. A new form and new way to protect the night."

Ahmik could not imagine what this new form might be, but loved the idea of still serving as a guardian. Thus, he followed the men as they led him to a small hut within the nearby forest.

"In here, boy," they gestured to the darkened entrance. "We kept your new shape safe inside here."

Had Ahmik been older, wiser in the ways of men and the world, perhaps he would have noticed the strange demeanor of the men. The way they shuffled their feet and averted their eyes; or even how their tone of voices shifted from placating to cajoling. As it was, Ahmik did not sense these things and with Muhe back in the sky, saw no other options.

It wasn't until he crossed the threshold of the small wikiup Ahmik realized his mistake.

The three men cheered and laughed at their cleverness as a lowly coyote exited the hut. It howled, a mournful sound, muzzle thrown back and up towards the sky. The men howled alongside him, mocking his naivety…Until they noticed the darkness around them beginning to recede.

Hearing the howl, Muhe had turned back to see the commotion and witnessed three men being cruel to the small woodland animal, kicking at it and throwing rocks. Thus she shined her light, weakened as it was, directly upon them. The flood of attention terrified the men. Fearing the consequences of their plot being discovered, they split and ran into the forest, leaving the coyote alone.

"There, there little one," Muhe cooed at the trembling creature. "They're gone now. You can run free."

When the little coyote didn't move, she continued, "Fear not, I will protect you. If they come back, if anything bad comes your way, just howl for my attention and you will have it."

At last the animal moved on, padding slowly away and shooting occasional glances back. Muhe resumed her nightly duties; eager to reclaim all she had missed while away.

Ahmik had done his best to get Muhe to understand, but his voice had been taken, replaced by the coyote's growl. With a heavy heart, he slunk off into the night, feeling the dirt beneath his paws and wondering at the sensation.

A "new way to protect the night" indeed! Though it was meant as a cruel joke, Ahmik would forever take his guardian duties seriously. He resolved to fulfill the task Naku had given him no matter the circumstances.

The night eyes the coyote form allowed him to still spot wickedness happening in the night. Wherever he spotted it, he would bring Muhe's attention to it. Thus, he took the men's words and made them his own; teaching the other coyotes to do the same.

Now it is said, when one hears the coyotes howl at the moon, rest assured that evil has been thwarted somewhere. Ahmik's service continues.

The Memories of a Non-Rez Kid

Sarah Martinez

Sarah Martinez

Hair

I've noticed that I do my hair like my mother.
Swept away into a clip in one fluid twist,
hiding all features and color.
An action so harmful to little me that even years away, she shudders.

Her hair, long and brown, flowing with an ease that took it years to
master. The red that only appears in the sun.
The grey that glints and shines.

She hates the grey—my favorite part.

So, the grey always went first;
pointing at her temples, she'd tell me which to pluck.
She'd tell me to pluck out her "Indian hairs"
to show me their strength.
She would tug and pull and tear against them,
boasting about their longevity.
I think she forgot the root kept them alive.
Maybe that's why I don't know about those who came before.
Each hair, a connection to an ancestor
that carried that strength and fervor.

She hates the wisdom, the love,
the story.
My father wasn't much better.
Bald.
His hair, once strong, curly Mexican hair,
Now buried under a tight layer of skin and bone,
speckled with skin cancer.
He's not all to blame; he's predisposed.

His father, also bald, held his language and story close to his chest.
He held it so tightly, it burned, and he resented it.
Not realizing he was only feeling his body heat.

I am anemic and always cold.
My hair is brown, curly, and strong.

I wish I could talk to my Grandpa and tell him to let go.
I wish my father could grow hair again.
I wish my mother believed in her beauty.
I wish that I could grey from my temples.

I hope I will grey from my temples.

An Unfinished Feeling

I have never met the same person twice—
with quirks, eye twitches, and hands that sew.
An established sense of self and style.
Now they see, they have no need to tiptoe.
But I am a mother, aunt, friend, father, and sister.
Behind cameras and white lies, I listen and look.
I wait for someone to find out my secret;
I am the mice in between the books.

The longer I'm silent, the bigger I grow.
Like foreign bugs leveling forests of trees.
Clones and copies that drop and scatter
like marbles on hardwood floors.
            Some, I'll never see again.
They immigrate into all parts of my life.
Two in love, four in family, and a thousand in knowledge.
They bounce and roll in my skull, serrated like knives.

The rolling it forms me,
I fold and give in.
Each day a reformee,
Weak and unwanted—

I see so many walls,
walls with vines and carvings.
I talk to these brick walls, all
while hoping to learn to harden overnight.

Childhood Friends

I think of plains, prairies, and trees.
Moderately gone. Forgotten.
Much like how the wind carries bees
down a path even they can't pin.
They miss the quiet, and so do I.
We are pushed further by what seems to be fate.
Away from a home, now too far to dance about.

Perhaps when they get back, it will have left, too.
Unable to bear the bee's departure.
Nature will pack herself into a city-shaped box.
The bees will wonder how all their flowers could ever fit.

The lizards and frogs that lived forever,
never left the homes that I made them.
Like Kudzu, they grow, unable to die,
not knowing what to do.
They may even grow jealous of me
and learn how to fly.
Maybe they'll find me floating along with the bees.

The Playdate

Silence that seeps in and brings out my loud,
for a playdate with yours.

They exchange words formally in a park or nice cafe
as their children (their more tender parts) meet happily
and scurry away.
The children both have brown hair that curls in the humidity.
They talk and laugh about songs and chase frogs,
while their older, rougher parts watch them
in a heavy, joyful silence
that can only be shared between almost friends.

Almost friends, stretched thinner than tissue,
scared a word will tear them apart forever.
But in this silence, the children play on

And in the silent watching,
we smile.

"Mended."

Mended, but unraveling.
The effort there and done, but
why show it?
What pride would come from it?
Use cheap thread on cheap clothes.
Use cheap thread on cashmere sweaters.

You sometimes have what you want, but
You put the box turtle in the lake
after finding him on the road,
knowing that to take care of him
is to put him somewhere outside,
but he doesn't breathe in the water.

Stupid and Ignorant.
Possibly undeserving.

Why? Do you think you'll remember
and opt for the forest next time?

Mending is who you are.
So, just mend.

Inheriting Fear

Jay D. Falcetti

When I was nine years old, I wanted nothing more than to get my ears pierced. I begged my father regularly. I explained I wanted to be like my older sister, to wear cubic zirconia and be fancy. Or I'd point to the young babies who had earrings and ask why I didn't get them then.

Each time I'd ask my dad, I'd get the same response—a simple but powerful "No."

My father was probably the smartest person I'll ever know. So, how do you appeal to someone who could basically predict the future based on their understanding of the human condition? Well, you wear them down with the continual asking. Don't assume, though, that the questioning does not come without repercussion.

At the time, I had only known life as a biracial Native kid growing up on a reservation on the northwest side of Arizona. I didn't know things could be safer or what "it doesn't have to be this way" meant.

What I knew was: I could never outsmart my father. He liked to drink—a lot; education was the answer to everything; and one white person in my family was enough.

On the night I finally reached the limit of inquiries, my father's eyes were glossy, and his stance leaned to the right. This was the father I knew, and I was going to get what I asked for.

He told me, "If you want your ears pierced, then I have to do it myself."

As I prefaced, I wanted nothing more, so I said, "Okay."

He grabbed my mother's sewing needle and held it over a small flame, the point licked by fire as I watched.

We didn't have ice cubes to numb my earlobes, he said. "Sometimes people use that for the pain."

When he placed his strong, calloused hand on my shoulder, I could barely swallow. My heart pounded until I could hear nothing else. My body trembling, I told him, "I'm scared."

He paused and studied my face for a moment before saying, "A great man once said, 'the only thing we have to fear is fear itself.' Do you know what that means?"

I shook my head no, and as he sighed, the acrid smell of alcohol drifted across my face.

"It means that you and you alone are creating that fear." He tapped my head. "It's in your head."

He pierced my ear, and I screamed. I could hear the crunch of my skin; the searing pain through my lobe made me sick to my stomach. My thoughts came to a screeching halt. I pushed his hand away and the needle with it.

Running to the corner of his bedroom, I covered my other ear and refused to let him pierce it. But that wasn't acceptable.

"People have been through far worse," he scolded. "They have real reasons to fear their fathers." He pulled me forward and forced me to my knees. He pierced the other side without my consent.

I dropped to the ground, crying, humiliated, with throbbing ears. My father bumped me with his foot and handed me a small bag with two earrings in it. "I got them from that Hopi lady who sells at IHS."

But I didn't want my ears to be pierced anymore; I didn't want to be near him. I wanted to run away.

Knowing my place, I grabbed the bag and squeezed it so hard the posts of the earrings stabbed me in the palm.

Seeing my disgust, he asked, "You want to see how easy this is?"

I didn't respond, tears salting my lips as he cleaned the needle with the flame again.

He put the needle in my hand. "Pierce my ear," he commanded.

Gingerly, I grabbed the needle and warned him, "This hurts," I whispered.

"No, it doesn't," he countered. "This is nothing. I'll show you."

Afraid of hurting my father, I hesitated.

"This isn't real pain." He glared at me, and I recognized that I needed to be careful—that I must pierce his ear.

So, I did—or I tried. I was shaking so badly I couldn't make it through the entire earlobe. I stretched his ear, trying to thin the flesh, but I still couldn't feel the needle on the other side. He never flinched, barely blinked. I thought he might be tired and apologized. He shrugged.

"At least you tried." He shooed me out of his room and shut the door behind me.

***

Several years later, my uncle died—my father's youngest brother. I was 12. As he sat in the living room, the misery he wore in his body made me nauseous. I'd never seen this side of my dad before.

This uncle had been my favorite. When I made a mistake, he would quickly and quietly correct my errors. Tying rebar together wrong? My uncle was there with a knife and a wink. He always had an extra candy bar in his pocket and was good for several tosses into the air. With him, I got to touch the sky.

I sat by my dad, waiting for him to ask me to do something—anything. When he spoke, the story he told stayed with me.

"My brother's dad shot himself in front of me. Right in the gut." My dad pointed to his, which was swollen with cirrhosis.

I didn't know what to say, or how to respond. I knew he was talking about my uncle's dad, whom my grandma later married after my grandfather passed away. This was long before my time, but important history he wanted me to know.

"I think about that day a lot," he mumbled.

"That must have been terrifying." my voice cracked.

He shook his head. "You don't know the meaning of terrifying."

A burst of anger caught in my chest. The ear piercing came to mind, but I held my tongue, and he took my silence as affirmation.

He continued, "I think about it because when I saw that blood pool on the ground, I ran outside looking for help." He side-eyed me. "Yeah, I was scared!" He flicked the top of his chew can, putting in a dip before his next words. "When I went into the yard, there just so happened to be a cop driving by. The timing—" He paused at the memory, speaking with a measured cadence. "It was so perfect. He was saved."

Tears welled in his eyes, but they didn't fall. He turned to me and asked, "Why couldn't my brother have that timing?"

We sat side by side in silence once more, watching television, both of us thinking about my uncle with vastly different memories.

I told myself I was lucky, that I was better off. I didn't experience anything like that, and I knew I never would. That night, before bed, I asked myself: do I truly know what it means to be terrified?

When I was 15, I asked him to pierce my nose—for him to be the one to do it. I made that request, but I never answered my question.

Creator Will Never Tell

Tommy Cheis

My boss, Dr. Demi Diaz, chair of the Psychiatry Department at Miami Jackson Behavioral Hospital, called as I raced west, dodging possum pancakes baking under a blazing sky on the griddle-hot Tamiami Trail. "Ina's grievously damaged by her five-year ordeal, Dr. Panther," she said.

"Thus her suicide attempt. It's my fault. I rescued her too late."

"No. Six weeks ago you saved her life. But you have to confront your wife with the truth, Jimmy. You're disappointed her love couldn't heal your war wounds. And now Ina's in danger."

"How? She was sedated when I left her bedside four hours ago."

"Security called Codes Blue, Grey, Black, and Orange. She's been kidnapped."

I nearly swerved into an onrushing police cruiser.

"By the cohort who trafficked her," Demi said, "starting with her mother, a/k/a the Witch, who approved the enterprise. And Ina's ex-husband, who sold her. Amon Rot."

"Tampa's chief of police."

"And Rot's pharmacist friend, who bought Ina and raped her ad infinitum in his dungeon. Don Olk."

I punched the steering wheel.

"And the psychopathic neighbor whose romantic advances Ina rebuffed. Anne Ilk."

My lip curled into a sneer. "The Owl. But why?"

"To shut her up permanently."

"Murder. Where did they take her?"

"Captiva Island, to ride out the hurricane. Hustle. Save your wife and my patient."

***

I snapped awake at the boat launch on Chokoloskee Island, then bolted from my car, jumped on *Wind*, the most powerful airboat in the world, and launched. Under brilliant moonwash, I passed waving sawgrass along the banks of the Lopez River, then plied into Crooked

Creek and clouds of seething gnats. Snapping turtles floated like mines in red mangroves. Raccoons, eyes aglow, hid behind bald cypress knobs, reporting my movement through territory to which they held title. Ancient organic stench hung above the murky brown water.

A half-hour into the trip, the "Slow Speed" sign appeared. I turned south. After ten minutes, I entered Sunday Bay, a body of water shaped like an equilateral triangle, illuminated by the warm orange glow of Crazy Harold's Huts set along a white sand beach. Barnacle-encrusted pilings sunk into marl held them just above water. Chickee roofs of woven palm fronds staved off sun and rain. On the deck of the command hut was a counter fashioned into a bar, standing racks of snacks, and a port-a-potty. I killed the engine, glided up, tied off, and climbed the ladder.

In a lawn chair by a plastic cooler, listening to a portable radio from which Gordon Lightfoot bemoaned that the feeling had gone and he just couldn't get it back, sat Harold Panther, ninety-three, my uncle, adoptive father, and the ugliest man in the world. A Chinese grenade tossed his way in Korea claimed his left eye and ear, half his tongue, and much jawbone. A descendant of Seminoles interned as prisoners-of-war in a fortress on Egmont Key, Harold sold his crate of medals to tourists for cash to start his moonshine distillery during the Kennedy administration.

And he was my everything. Shortly before I was born, my father, a descendant of Chiricahua interned in Pensacola who escaped, ran south, and mingled with the Seminole, took a panther for ceremonial purposes. The game warden dismissed his Native sovereignty defense. My father, who'd raped me into Harold's daughter, killed four deputies before he was subdued. The State of Florida fried him a week before my first birthday. One year later, barbiturates, vodka, and a razor claimed my mother. She left no note. I fished a Red Stripe from the cooler, popped the top, and handed it Harold, apologizing for my tardiness.

He scoffed. "Ain't no time at tha origin," he said. "Glad ya here." He lip-pointed east. "Killer storm comin. Nineteen hour off."

"I know. I came to get you. And I need your help."

"Nah. Ya fine by ya self. Ina however. She been kidnap." He guzzled his brew.

I thought I'd dreamt it in a driving-induced microsleep. My heart lurched. My vision swam.

"Come as a shock, eh? Figgered." Harold crushed the can one-handed. "Just do same ya did on tha playground when ya whipped tha asses a that gang attackin her on tha monkey bars."

"Uncle, Ina and I were nine then. I gave up violence long ago."

"Ha! Say tha man got hisself covered in ribbons fa what he did in tha war."

"I've changed."

"Change back. Them folks what hurt Ina afore ya come back inta her life need killin."

"Look where killing got my dad. I just want peace."

"Shit. Peace only come when tha fightin's done. N ya so fuckin good at fightin."

I said nothing.

Harold spat. "But if ya want out, just take off runnin n never come back. Find a cosmic fuckin rationale ta dodge ya duty."

"Like a psychiatrist I'm supposed to help people, not hurt them?"

"Psychiatrist don't mean shit in tha real world. N Hippocrates can fuck hisself. Ya gotta hurt some ta hep others. Ina n ya unborn. Creator asking who matter ta ya, n who in fuck are ya?"

"So this is all a test?"

"Yep. N all ya can do is fill in bubbles as problems come at ya. Creator'll tally up ya score."

"I don't believe in ghost stories," I lied. Lightning flickered.

"Ha!" Harold smacked an adjacent chair, then hawked into the creek. A catfish burst from the murky water to vacuum his sputum. Harold laughed into paroxysms and went blue.

I jumped up to assist.

He pushed me off with ease, then launched into some old fable. "Way back, tha Chiricahua was threaten by Monsters."

"I know the origin story, Uncle. Child-of-Water slew Buffalo, Eagle, Antelope, then Elk."

His glare withered me. "Monsters I'm talkin bout, accordin to ya daddy," he continued, "was Evil Ones killin Chiricahua in tha Chiricahua Mountains. Spaniards prolly. Seventeen century. An a *diyyin* begged Usen ta hep."

"A Chiricahua medicine leader."

"Usen say run quick. Get on tha tallest mountain. So Chiricahua sit three days n nights n no water. Day four, Wind blow out tha West. Lightning slash out tha North. Thunder barrel out tha East. Sun rise out tha South. Then Sun, Wind, Thunder, n Lightnin hug n shout '*Hookah*!'

"Translated, 'Let's go!'"

"They join arms n spin counterclockways, eh? Then they rotate arms n charge, suckin Water off Ocean. Black Cloud wrap em up n they fly over *Nde benah*."

"Land of the People."

"Mmm. As Black Cloud sail cross Sky, Day become Night. Water is seethin white foam. Chaos everwhere. When Sun, Wind, Thunder, n Lightnin arrive, too late fa Evil Ones ta climb."

I was riveted.

"Then Sun depart. Black Cloud thicken. Evil Ones run but Wind blow four direction. Chiricahua start singin Wind Song." He sang the old words: *Let it be well, my brother Wind. Blow wide. Continue in a good way. Do not harm your poor people but do your duty against the Evil Ones.*

I was transfixed.

"Then Wind blow down tha Evil One, wrench em limb ta limb, n toss corpses. But no Chiricahua hurt. Now Lightnin strike out four direction. So Chiricahua sing Lightnin Song." And so did Harold. *Let it be well, my brother Lightning. Strike high. Continue in a good way. Do not harm your poor people but do your duty against the Evil Ones.*

Something stirred in me.

"Then Lightnin burn Evil Ones ta ash," he said.

"Were any Chiricahua hurt, Uncle?"

"Nah. So Thunder boom out four direction, n Chiricahua sing Thunder Song." As did he: *Let it be well, my brother Thunder. Clap all around us. Continue in a good way. Do not harm your poor people but do you duty against the Evil Ones.*

I felt Power.

"Then Thunder boom, Jimbo, blowin Evil Ones ta bits."

"But leaving the Chiricahua unmolested?"

"Man, woman, child. Then Child-a-Water return to earth. In a shirt a abalone. Chiricahua sing Child-a-Water Song." And he repeated it: *Let it be well, Child-of-Water. Wash all around us. Continue in a good way. Do not harm your poor people but do your duty against the Evil Ones*. "So Child-a-Water unleash deluge," he said. "Evil Ones drown. *Nde benah* purified. Chiricahua saved. You trackin?"

I twitched in anticipation, but shrugged.

Harold spat. "All ya see's an old man flappin lips, eh? I ain't inspired ya. Well, listen up. Ya own Evil Ones is pressin ya. N a storm comin. N history repeats herself."

Lightning flashed. I faced myself, then Harold. "Uncle, please sing again."

"Ya know who ya are now?"

" I think I always have."

We sang together until I knew the songs better than Ina's face. Harold abruptly quit mid-verse. "Time ta rescue Ina. She in tha Witch compound. Got two floor. Like a igloo made a titanium Legos two foot thick. N they's a giant steel safe upstairs."

"A sealed panic room with its own generators and oxygen so you can survive a hurricane?"

Harold grunted. "Least tha front half. T'Evil Ones gone be inside. Panickin."

"Good. How do I open the door?"

"Just wish it so. Sun ain't risin today. Don't got no three days ta wait. *Wind*'ll get ya there and back with Ina aboard. Hustle."

***

I was one with the hurricane, pure of arms. We grew deadlier even as we rode up onto the beach dragging foam and chaos behind, scouring Captiva Island clean down to the coral save for the compound. *Wind's* bow stopped before a gaping maw in the compound where we'd wrenched away sliding glass doors, casements, and shutters. Orion shone. Mars reigned.

I clambered over the gunwale and ran inside. Two feet of water filled the first floor, but none cascaded from the second. Upstairs windows were intact. I felt my way up the central staircase and found Ina nude in the corner of an open room. Her jaw smashed. Her face flattened. Her eyes glazed and sightless. A sharp effusion of crimson and the remainder of our unborn child coagulated on the tile. I checked her pulse but she was cool and stiffening.

I tore out my hair, laid on the floor, held her, and bawled. Hours passed before I could say goodbye to all that had tethered me to this world.

Then my true nature returned at a gallop. Time slowed, compressed, stopped.

I rose and gathered myself. The backup generator kicked in. Eerie bloodred emergency lights flicked on along the second floor ceiling. I hustled to the panic room and willed the door open.

The circular portal, ten feet of chromium steel across, pivoted.

The pale white faces of the Evil Ones stared back at me.

The Owl—a short round greasy woman—screamed. She wore jeans, a flannel, duckboots, a necklace of little metal birds of Minerva, and hid her mouse-blond hair under a red bandana.

I greeted the four. "What a foul assemblage. Justice mandates consequences for bad acts."

The Witch—a rotund septuagenarian—grabbed the Owl's hand. The wicked sisters ran to the rear of the wedge-shaped room.

Don, the pharmacist, chased after them.

Rot—with an arrogant sneer, folded teeth, and slouched shoulders—jiggered an interior panel.

The door swung shut.

I willed it open again.

Rot jumped forward, pistol in hand, and fired.

I jerked sideways.

Rot fired again and again, emptying the magazine.

I dodged all his bullets.

"I sent a BOLO before the storm arrived, Jimmy," Rot shouted from the rear of the panic room. "When they catch you, you'll die in Old Sparky like your daddy."

"Wrong. I'm immortal."

"They said you were crazy!" Rot yelled. "Even for a shrink! SWAT will be here in twenty minutes!"

"Wrong, Chief. The roads are underwater. Power lines hang like spaghetti. Your goons won't beat the back half of the storm."

The truth sank into Rot. "Let's talk, Dr. Panther."

"Dr. Panther's absent. Child-of-Water's here."

"We have money," he offered, oblivious to who I was. "I mean Ina's mother can get it. Let us go and I won't file charges," he offered as if to sweeten things. "Afterward, complete disengagement. Just take the money."

"Nah. All the world's cash is pennies on the dollar you owe Ina. You'll pay for your transgressions in flesh. You each owe Ina a death. I'm here to collect."

"Why you?" the Owl simpered.

"Because of my provenance. You executed horrid crimes against my people. Kidnapping. Rape. Murder. Let's talk order of operations. I'll attend you sequentially. Choose the order yourselves, or I will. You get five minutes to palaver. *Hookah*. Let's go."

"What gives you the right?" the Witch snarled, still haughty and unresigned to her fate.

"I was created for this."

Downstairs, I found a floating bucket containing dark grouting paste.

Upstairs, I fingerpainted. On one wall, I made the Chiricahua symbol for Sun. On another, the symbol for Cloud. On a third, the symbol for Wind. On a fourth, Lightning. On the ceiling I painted Water, Stars, Water, and Sun, finishing the epic cycle. Time for the blood sacrifice.

I went to the panic room and opened the door. "It's time, you Evil Ones. Who's on first?"

Rot tossed the Owl tumbling through the door.

I cracked knuckles. "Greetings, Owl."

Her eyes were glassy. I doubt she heard me.

"In the Divine Comedy," I lectured, "Dante Alighieri outlines punishment for Hypocrites. Those who feign virtue yet are in fact wicked liars. Have you read it?"

She wouldn't or couldn't speak. Fear has that effect.

I dragged her downstairs and onto the beach and resumed. "In serious cases, Hypocrites were whipped, their eyes were burnt out, and, decked in leaden robes, they were flung into the sea."

Life crept back into the Owl. "I d-don't d-deserve this."

"No? Unrequited love is toxic. If you'd let it go rather than conspiring to have Ina trafficked and raped, you'd be safe abed."

"Ina's a liar. And I didn't rape her."

"But you did, vicariously. You brokered an oxy for rape scheme between Ina's addict ex-husband, the chief of police, and your childhood pal, Don the pharmacist. Then you cloaked it in the narrative that Don was crazy Ina's caretaker. Then you secured the approval of Ina's mother, a severe antisocial personality who's hated Ina from the moment she was born. Even if Ina had been able to escape without my help, who'd have believed her tale? Your agglomeration of evil was the perfect insurance policy to get all your needs met."

"Don and Rot ran the whole thing."

"They'll get what's coming to them too. Everyone does eventually."

"If you hadn't come along, none of this would be happening. Let me go, asshole."

"Where? The island will be under twenty feet of water in forty minutes. The compound has structural damage. It won't survive the second half. You're all dying today. Only question is—how?"

The Owl screwed up her face. "Ina deserved to be raped!"

I grabbed her by the hair and dragged her to the ocean's lip.

The far side of the eye was visible. Thick, boiling, angry clouds.

I pinched her nose, grabbed her tongue with pliers, and sliced it out.

She babbled nonsensically, but at last spoke the truth.

I pulled weight belts from a compartment on *Wind,* affixed them around her neck and knocking knees, then rolled her face down, dragged her to sea, and released her.

I ran for the compound. Halfway there, I snuck a look.

Dorsal fins whirred explosively, cycling a bloodred gyre in the water.

I grabbed a line, then ran to the kitchen. In the detritus of shattered cabinets I dug up a garbage bag. I shoveled ice from the freezer bin with my hands until the bag was half-full, then ran upstairs, found an office chair, wheeled it to the panic room, and opened the door.

Rot, the Witch, and Don cowered in a state of fear-induced helplessness.

"Who's next?" I barked.

No one uttered a sound.

"In ten seconds I'm coming in, kids. Last chance for democracy."

Rot twisted the Witch's arm behind her back and bulldozed her out of the circle and under the bloodred lights.

I pushed the Witch to the staircase, tossed her over my shoulder, and kicked the chair clattering downstairs. Then I dragged her by the collar into the kitchen.

She glowered like a possessed eagle pursuing the panther that ate her eaglets. "How dare you burst into my home uninvited and behave this way?"

"I'm here on a mission to rescue my wife and kill you all."

"Ina needed no rescue. I told you—she lies."

"As she did when she came to you and reported your husband for raping her in childhood?"

The Witch glimmered with glee. "Ina's always been a drama queen. Don was her caretaker. And a doctor," she dissembled stubbornly.

I grabbed the ice bag and cut the rope to the proper length. "Wrong," I said. "Don was a Walmart pharmacist who tortured and raped her at your behest. Now he's my prisoner."

Her eyes blazed. "Don did what he could. Ina lost her mind when Amon rejected her like every other man has."

"Wrong, Ina filed to divorce Amon five years ago because he planned to sell her to Don with your approval. And I didn't reject her. You did. Now your daughter's dead."

The Witch harumphed. "Let Don go this instant."

I shook my head in disbelief. "I repeat: Ina's dead. And her unborn baby too."

The Witch's eyes slitted. "Good. The thought of a half-breed baby sickens me. Ina brought everything on herself."

I gnashed my teeth. "You call yourself a Christian. Do you believe in hell?"

"Certainly. That's where you're going."

"Then I'll give you a thirty-minute head start. Fire or ice?"

"Whatever do you mean?"

"You denied choice to Ina. I'm more generous. You get to pick how you'll die."

The Witch tried to kill me with her eyes. "You're evil, James Panther."

"Child-of-Water."

"If you hadn't come along, none of this would be happening."

"So I've heard. Time's up. Ice will suffice." I tied the bag with two loops of rope around her neck. She went into shock. I pushed her outside to face the storm's wrath. Two down. Two to go.

From my boat, I took hammer, nails, pyro putty, and a lighter.

Back inside, I found a bathroom, tapped drywall to find a hollow space, kicked, and pulled two four-by-six boards each ten feet long.

Outside, I nailed them together, laid the cross on the sand, and dug a pit by the incoming tide.

***

The panic room door swung out. Rot and Don rushed me.

Rot tried to dart past on my right. I clotheslined him. A wet thwap of meat against meat as he went down, larynx bruised, writhing.

I turned on Don. He was an inch or two shorter than I—rangy, with a carpet of graying hair on his visible body. He stunk of rotten gym shoes, sewage, and offal, and pulsed with the energy of an admixture of evils from a dreadful place beyond the grave. I twitched in anticipation of the kill.

But before I closed the distance, Don zipped back into the panic room. The door closed.

So Rot would be third. I tied rope around his ankle and dragged him downstairs. His head hit every cement step.

At the cross on the beach, I dropped the rope and knelt. He was groggy. When he took in the cross and its accoutrement, he struggled lamely to rise.

"You won't get away with this, Panther," he said, mindless of the cliché.

"Child-of-Water."

"You're crazy."

"We're all as crazy as hell. What defines us is whether we channel insanity for good or ill. It's a sequence, Rot. The Owl died as Black Cloud blocked the Sun. Wind will gather sand and flay the Witch from her bones. Lightning is your terminus. For Don, Water. First, I have questions. Why did you marry Ina?"

"To pass and have kids."

"Why let her go?"

"She was useless after popping the second kid. Lavender marriages suck. I did it for my mother."

"Why not get an amicable divorce instead of trafficking her?"

"There's opportunity in every crisis. And I always hated her." He put a hand on his head as if it was the cap of an electric chair, then pulled back his eyelids with his fingertips, mocking my father who, like Rot, had had it coming. "Dipshit," he branded me. "Egg-bearers are everywhere. What do you see in Crazy Ina?"

"She wasn't crazy. She was traumatized from five years in your rape camp. Now she's dead."

Rot smirked. "We all do whatever we can get away with. Take it up with Don."

I punched him unconscious, rolled him onto the cross, grabbed his left hand, stretched his arm, centered a nail between radius and ulna, then swung the hammer. The nail pierced the joint. Blood spurted. I repeated the process. Once his arms were affixed to the crossbar, I pulled his legs straight and drove a nail between the metatarsals of each foot. Then I lifted the cross and dragged the top of the beam into the pit. Rot was crucified upside down, feet pointed skyward. I drew my knife, sliced the flesh under his ribcage, and let his viscera, under the influence of gravity, spill onto the sand.

Rot never got the chance to scream. I arranged pyro putty under his head, but before I could flick the lighter, ZZZZZZZZZ!

Lightning had struck. I was as if I'd flown too close to the sun. I was unscathed, but Rot was charred to cinders. His reeking remainder, pushed by a sudden puff of wind, toppled to the sand.

Embers glowed. Sparks flew.

Wind pelted the unconscious Witch and dispersed Rot's ashes. Three down.

But the apotheosis of evil remained. For Don, it would be full Hammurabi.

I stood with arms outstretched, legs wide, in the circular opening of the panic room, waiting for the panic to fully bloom.

After a while, Don, blubbering, spoke to fill the terrifying void. "S-s-say something!!"

I said nothing.

He began a silent rash of shuddering sobs.

"You and I cannot both live on this earth," I explained after a while.

"P-please," he begged. "S-Spare m-my l-life."

"Can't. I'm obliged to take it from you as you use it so badly."

He sank to his haunches and hiss-whispered, "You're no killer. You're too good a person to do this."

"Wrong. I'm the cruelest, most unforgiving creature ever sung into being. You should know that. You're my Creator." I went in and knelt next to him.

His eyes were a blend of lichens, bile, and infected mucus. He was big and strong enough to terrify any woman, but his prime malignancy was immaterial, extraordinary, and from eons past. The menace and venom instantiating him were distilled from ancient atavisms buried so deep beneath the sea of humanity that in just one in ten million births did they ooze to the surface.

"You," I told him, "should never have done what you did to a woman with a husband as good at killing as I am."

He sobbed. "P-p-please d-don't k-kill m-me." His bowels evacuated. Urine dripped down his leg and puddled. The room took on a barnyard tang. He held out his hands as if to embrace.

"I have to, Don. It's my reason for being."

Don hoot-panted like a chimpanzee, then issued a hideous moan halfway between foghorn and yoga chant. Then he stutter-whispered, calling me a brute and an ogre. Then he went catatonic.

"You thought Ina was the perfect victim," I said. "No husband to rescue her. No family. No friends. Prior rape history. On the autism spectrum and unable to get help. Nod yes. Shake no."

He nodded and sobbed.

"And you thought yourself safe to run your rape camp until you killed her. Today, you did. I'm curious. If you'd known of me, would you have behaved differently?"

He hesitated, then slowly peeled back his lips into a smirk as if work was done and it was party time. "Never," he hissed. "Ina wrote you years ago." He was wooden and eerie. Something had awakened. "But you did nothing. Years passed without a phone call or email. Nod yes. Shake no."

He'd turned the tables. I nodded despite myself.

"No one gave a shit. Including you," he taunted. "When you showed faint flickers of interest but blew her off, we thought you a coward. Or homosexual. Or both. Your neglect bought time for me to ruin Ina for all other men." He spoke calmly, with perfect diction.

"I've heard and read about your deeds."

He grinned. "But you had to be there to appreciate them. And her wails. Her screams. Her blood. Did you know, in the adjacent room, I raped her for the three hundredth time? What a milestone. I counted. Carefully. And I've tortured and raped many others."

"You're a monster."

He beamed. "I worked hard to merit that distinction. Thanks. Do you know, I believe I raped your child out of Ina entirely?"

Outside, the roar of a diesel train engine from hell deepened in pitch.

"Relax," he said. "The abortion's free. As a pharmacist, I'm part of your medical family. Give us a kiss, Jimmy."

Something broke inside me. "Are those the eyes that first saw Ina?"

He grinned. "As God beholds a sinning whore."

"Did those teeth scar her?"

He clapped in glee. "You've seen my work? I'm a body artist among my many talents."

"Which hand grabbed Ina's throat?"

"Both. Her hyoid nearly snapped."

I pointed to his ears. "Those heard her screams?"

"Ina has excellent theatrical pitch."

"Is that the nose that smelled her perfume?"

"And her fear. The signature scents of my home until you stole my luxurious plaything."

"Pull out your cock."

He did. "Now suck it."

I ignored the goad and pointed to the little flesh nub. "Is that what you used to rape Ina?"

"Deep in her triune holes, including her asshole, asshole."

I unsheathed my knife and held it by the tip.

He beheld the blade and sniggered.

"Take it," I insisted, "and drag the razor edge across your wrists. It's easier than what I've prepared for you."

He laughed. "Like you didn't let the other three go."

"The back half of the hurricane will be on us any minute. Where do you think your colleagues went?"

He shrugged. "A car. A boat. You're just trying to scare me."

"How do you want it? Blood loss? Drowning? Both?"

He looked at the blade as if it were his next victim, laid the fingers of his good hand on the handle, then hesitated.

"Come on, Don. Dispatch me and walk free."

His hand fell to his lap. "For maybe ten minutes, until the second half of the storm arrives."

"Maybe five. But the pain would be less. Otherwise the interval to come will be hard for you."

He smiled. "I'll ride it out in here just fine."

"The compound won't survive the back half of the hurricane. Kill yourself, or I'm going to waltz you through a wonderland worse than death."

"You wouldn't. You're a pussy."

"Want to bet?" I slapped the knife into his hand.

He dropped the blade.

I looped a noose around his neck and jerked him up.

He shrieked. "WHAT ARE YOU DOING?!"

"Executing the ancient law of man."

"OH! I'M SORRY! OH GOD! PLEASE FORGIVE ME!"

I sliced off his ear. The tissue separated as a lettuce leaf peels from the head.

He skirled in agony then prayed. "Hail Mary, full of grace, the Lord is with thee; blessed art thou among women, and..."

I sliced off his other ear, then kicked him wall-to-wall. "Admit you like this and I'll stop."

Don went frantic. "Holy Mary mother of God, pray for us sinners now and at the hour of—"

I removed his nose. A bloody mucilaginous slime ran hot and wet down his face and garbled his words. I pummeled his face. Bones cracked. He puked, then wore a death mask. I kept on, went deaf to the sounds he made, and hammered out teeth. Two stuck in my hand. I flicked them away, then stuck my blade a quarter-inch through his eyelids.

Clear fluid leaked onto his cheeks.

I hacked off both index fingers and tossed them behind me.

He keened and wailed. My very own banshee.

I sawed off his penis and testicles.

He bled front and back and moaned like a dying cow.

I bit his back to shreds, then dragged him downstairs. I sharpened a closet pole into a spear, then dragged him onto the sand near Rot's crucifixion.

"Are you ready for the finale?" I asked the final Monster.

No response.

Water reclaimed the seabed. Earth shook. Wind flung sand, abrading flesh from the Witch's bones. Lightning slashed cloud-to-cloud. My hair stood. I smelled ozone. Balls of blue flame rolled from south to north, trailing fire with their passage. Inside the onrushing eyewall, flames crackled.

I inserted my spear in Don's anus, rammed until two feet disappeared, then dragged him until the blunt spear end slid into the pit and set him upright. He made not a sound.

Water rushed higher until he was submerged, then gone.

It was done. The cycle was complete.

But I'd failed. Chiricahua had died and I wanted to join them.

I ran back upstairs and waited for the end with Ina.

But the hurricane abated. Stars came out. After a while, the sun rose.

"Always been a gap between story n practice," I heard Harold say from far off. "Kid, ya know who ya are now n ya done what ya could. Proud a ya."

Gripping that razor-sharp sawgrass stalk hard enough to draw blood, I sang Ina into *Wind* and back to Harold. That night, sadder and wiser, singing of Sun, Cloud, Wind, Lightning, and Water, we buried her where white men will never go and Creator will never tell.

Voices of the Caribbean

Dark Moon

Brian Jose Welch

Paganism's Delight

As they look upon my life's clouds
they scatter black ashes.
"Make them rain a shower of destruction," they say.
You are always amused of our setbacks
with wicked whips on our backs,
into our lives.
I saw stepping stones on our sorrow to see your wicked salvation.

But I will never miss their target in any language,
when I call upon the Lord.
However, your studies inspire many to do your dirty works.
Let me not love your dark arts,
because there are many that rose up the waters of evil against me.

Equity leaves will flourish upon the accursed soil,
which is piled up with corruption and strife
but let me get the good broom of god
and his holy flame of a lighter to burn it all!

Hopeless Nomad

Crossing Hell's Bridge, I feel anxious
to reach a cool place to rest.
As I fly through the never-ending dimensions of a false reality,
I began to look upon the truth,
which hides behind cloudy walls.
But I search for a solution to this weary,
yearning to destroy this obstacle, which I found to be me.
Just as a child finding his rest after long days of adventures,
I will ascend back into the covetable heaven's pillar
that reminds me of goodness,
that I cherished with open palms.
But do not let me forget this world that made me witness
the different winds of wonder that blow in human time,
but let that eternal moon shine on its children's face
for all eternity.

Many adversities of spiritual demons hunt me
in many lands of horror
Hatred,
Heinous,
and hypocrisy.
But your love creates a black barrier
to bring back my immortal lost soul.

Your permanent thorns of hatred
lies deep beneath a terrible surface
that even love hands can take out.
Let not the bruises and scars of treachery
create a persona, a pure hatred for mankind,
but hold their hands though their storms of sins
to see the bright skies of your shining love.

The Second First Woman: A Corocote Story

N.O. Gomez Flores

Hundreds of Taino men stood at the shore of the Island without Women, which as of two minutes ago was the Island with Men and a Pretty Normal Amount of Women. Guahayona rowed away in his big *canoa*, laughing, all the women looking back at the lives he made them leave.

"You'll never fuck again, hahahaha!" yelled one of the men, screaming back at him.

He started towards the water, sure he could swim faster than a canoe if sex was on the line, but stopped when the shallow waves stunted his run. Another came to pick him up as he kneeled crying. The two brothers suffered watching the escape party that the entirety of the women on the island and the cacique had planned months ago. This was evidenced by the lack of struggle from the women. In fact, now that one of the brothers thought about it, they were in fact laughing and enjoying the escape like a good Sunday boat ride. The men stood for a moment. They were by their sons, bawling for their lost mothers. Most of the children were crying on the ground, less than most of them leaped to the forest behind. Further and further, the canoa left little by little. At the edge of the horizon, the hand of one of the big guys upstairs cracked the sky and took the false cacique, leaving the boat full of confused women adrift.

"What do we do now?" asked one.

His brother, equally stunned by the sight, replied, "I know a guy."

The brothers, along with a few dozen men stood in front of a guy he knew. Although to describe this guy as being a "guy" would be misleading. This on account of the "guy" being composed of two beautiful black wings stemming from a crisp white chest that matched a white mask he wore and a beak so sharp, it would inspire a future Urayo'Keno to up his stick point game. The guy was also a full ten inches tall and very nervous, as he now stood in front of a few dozen Taino and had his leg rudely tied to a tree.

His name was Inriri, famous for banging his head really hard against wooden things, then flying off and banging his head on other wooden things some more. His gaze twitched from Taino to Taino, all who waited for the older brother, the one who knew the guy, to speak. The brother did not. His bird-speak was almost nonexistent and limited to screaming at the *pitirre* bird, to leave him be. Instead, they spoke the long-revered language of international peoples, pointing at stuff and kind of imitating what he wanted. He waved to Inriri, touched his hand with his finger, then pointed at a tree, and touched his hand with his finger a little faster now. Inriri didn't understand and could not reply as he did not have the fingers to reciprocate. The Taino were getting frustrated after a few minutes of this. Some put their palm on their face, others walked back to their all-male *yukayeques*, which means town in other, less fun languages.

Without waiving a word, the younger brother picked up Inriri, turned him around, and put him back down in front of a rather nice caoba tree. Inriri started immediately to fly and look for a spot on this strange tree to bang his head on. Two lumps a bit higher up looked like a good place to get a spacious home and grub, but after drilling a tiny hole in each one, he found them too soft to be of any use. The *tokotokotoko* had a few Taino heads turn back as they walked away, but it was the sight of the closest thing to a pair of breasts they'd seen since a couple of hours ago that helped turn the rest of their body around. It was rudimentary, wooden, but what a sight for starved eyes. Enough to buy the rest of the afternoon to stay watching. This would be the time of day where they'd be miles away hunting game, sharing stories between foliage. But half of their yukayeque was gone, so they had a pretty good amount of resources to take the day off this once.

Inriri mesmerized the men, as he masterfully banged a bit of wood with furious indecision before going to another spot of the tree to bang a bit more. So impressive was his work that a whispered crack in the sky opened to a pair of eyes peering through. Slowly, through beak bangs, a beautiful splintered body stared at their gleaming eyes. Its feet draped still over the base of the caoba, running up etched legs almost crossed over. The asymmetrical hips were covered by blocky slim arms that ended in a beautiful flat face looking up into the trunk that sprouted to a leafed sky. Inriri panted, wings hanging, thin tongue halfway out of his brain. He rested between the two soft lumps he'd rejected before.

Only the forest spoke. The brother who knew the guy stood proudly next to his guy's work. The eyes in the broken sky brought up Guahayona to marvel at the people he betrayed.

In the stunned crowd, a timid Ereyi stuttered, "It's, um, it's missing something."

The brother who knew a guy glared at him, terrified that his new rise to cacique had fallen short after all these hours of proudly standing next to his diminutive hostage. Inriri slurped his tongue in upon hearing the possibility of more forced labor and darted into the sky, only for his tiny ankle to remember the string that had so lovingly embraced it. The speed at which Inriri flew met with the tension arched him straight into a rock that was a long-string-and-tied-bird away from the tree. The group looked at the smashed Inriri with spread wings on the ground. The group looked at Ereyi.

"What the Juracan, Ereyi?" asked one of the men.

Ereyi looked at his feet. A couple more eyes looked down through the crack in the sky.

The brother who used to know a guy tapped his foot with arms crossed. He wanted an answer but was too furious to even ask it.

Another man stated, "He made tiny holes for the nipples, and her eyes look so beautiful. And, um, he made her mouth perfect. Open and everything! She can hear herself speak because he made her ears holes too!"

The brother was not satisfied with all the compliments, but they did stop his foot.

"But, um, I just mean that, well. How is she supposed to pee?" asked someone.

The group on the ground and the group through the sky looked at the Brother who used to know a guy. Guahayona laughed uncontrollably between the giant fingers that held him. This oversight helped fulfill his last words to the men when he left on the canoa.

The brother muttered, "Shit!"

He grabbed the limp body of the guy he knew, a rock, and went to town between the body's legs. It was not a pretty sight, most would even say a very small bloody one. But to an extent, it honored the little Inriri to bang his head on wood one last time. With splished sounds, he chipped away and made three new holes between the statue's legs. He really wasn't too sure how many the usual women had, having never been with one; but he was sure it was at least two. One more for good measure, and none more because, by then, Inriri's head was a bloody splat on the middle one.

Every mouth was agape. This blocky splintered form was beautiful in the same way getting home from school at 4:00 pm, laying on your *hamaca*, and putting on Los Simpsons was beautiful. At least to the *tona* who leapt into the bushes to spy on their dads. To the fathers, it was beautiful in the way seeing an anatomically accurate wooden statue of a woman's body a few hours after every woman you know vanishes into the horizon is beautiful. All of the women upstairs watching through the sky scoffed at the wonder this Island Without Women had, and Inaguaboina, very much in suit for her short temper, zapped the figure with a large, pink thunder. The men screamed in prayer to ask why she took the closest thing to a woman they thought they'd have.

The Brother, who squashed a guy he knew, ran away stumbling between the wailing men. As the glittery dust settled, the Taino racquet collectively became an ohhhh as the figure stood naked in front of them, blinking her eyes rapidly at her first sight of, well, anything. Her skin kept the copper tinge of the *caoba* evergreen, she was carved from. She had straight, black hair draped over shrugged shoulders and a terrified expression of the newly acquired burden of existence.

"What hap-" blurted his brother.

A second, almost less pink, and definitely smaller thunder hit her right in the throat.

"Sando?" called one man.

By now none of the men made sound nor movement. Each minute passing was stranger than the one before. The second first woman kept darting her eyes to every object as if it was new in terrifying; an action rooted in the fact that she had never seen anything ever and every object was equally terrifying. Iguanaboina looked down on them with contempt in her gigantic eyes, all that could be seen through the crack.

The more the woman saw, the more her feet shifted. She tried finding a very good place to bury something of her that'd make her feel less of this really bad feeling she had. She didn't know what she could bury or what this bad feeling was, but it was very much something she did not like. Ereyi was the only one to move, carefully putting one foot in front of the other, with his chest low to his knees, arms out. He wanted her to know that he was very small and not a threat and, if she so wanted, a very soft thing she could hug and hide on. The woman upstairs grunted long enough to become a guttural scream confusing his teddy bear interpretation for a hunting one. In her fury, sent a barrage of thunder that struck the woman and every tree that stood around them. Not every tree, the number of attacked trunks was exactly the amount of men that were on the island plus one. It was a loud, deafening, short-lived thunderstorm; but in terms of volume, it was very mild in comparison to the cacophony of women that now ran around trying to understand what was happening and where they were.

The men were already jumping into the water, running to the yukayeque, hiding under any sufficiently hideable rock. The group looking through the sky stared judgingly at the proud Iguanaboina, smirking at her chaos.

"Mooooooooom.", screamed Yucahu.

The *iguanaboina* scrambled off the sky window, closing the rift before Atabey, mother of all gods, saw what she did. An unidentified hand upstairs opened it a bit again, touched every woman's head at the same time then closed it back up.

On the island, a few of the women screamed long enough to figure out they could understand each other. The trees became the commanding silence again, and the women began walking toward the yukayeque. On the way, the second first woman spoke to her sisters telling them about the amazing adventures she had in seconds that she was the only woman not on a canoa in the middle of the sea. She didn't know a lot, so the tales were short. It was fortunate, then, that the tree the men had chosen to make her from was fairly close to town. The sight of the round-roofed huts—the *bohios*—filled them with warmth as if they knew this was their home. At the entrance of the yukayeque, a very worried Ereyi paced back and forth looking at the ground. He mumbled and grunted thinking about the events just passed, stopping in his tracks at an army of nude women of every age marching straight at him. The second first woman recognized him, she knew he'd tried to help her before. She wasn't sure how, since the moment he got close to her, a hundred other hers appeared. Still, this was a trustworthy person. The caring man stood before her, and every woman existing stood in front of him.

Ereyi touched his chest and said "Ereyi", because that is what his name was.

"Eyeri," mispronounced the second first woman to her sisters, because she thought it meant man.

Eieri misunderstood the mass of women as they walked into their new lives.

Voices of Africa

The Heirloom

Solape Adetutu Adeyemi

1. The Heirloom

I am the quiet witness,
passed from hand to hand,
kept through life and death.
My surface is dull,
my edges smooth
from the touch of many hands.
Hands searching for meaning,
for a piece of the past.

I was made long ago,
shaped by someone
you have forgotten,
but his blood is in yours.
The first to hold me,
holding me tight.
For he needed me to matter.

I went through war,
hidden in a pocket,
close to his beating heart.
I felt his fear—
his courage—
until silence came.
Then I became a memory,
kept in a wooden box
with the smell of tears.

I have felt joy, too.
A mother's hands,
giving me to her child.
I have been at weddings,

heard laughter,
and the sound of love turning to anger,
words sharp like broken glass.
I know regret.
It clings to me like rust.

I have seen families grow,
then shrink.
Homes become quiet,
faces fade into memories.
Now, you hold me.
Your hands are like theirs,
though you don't know my story.
But it doesn't matter.
You are here,
and I am here.

I keep the truth of your family,
its love and loss,
its strength and struggle.
I stay the same,
but you change.
Still, I remain.

2. When I Left

And when I left,
I left the pain, the containment, the worry,
the anguish, and the insults.
And I thought I had left for good,
but I forgot
to leave my memories behind.

3. Jalopy

You must always remember—
we were there for you when no one else was.
We contributed money for your education,
and when you were done,
we even contributed money for the jalopy you drive.
Some of us own the steering wheel.
Some of us own the tyres.
Some of us own the dashboard.
The seats plus the seat belts!
Even the engine!
The brakes and accelerator—inclusive!
Just so you remember,
we own you.

4. Visually Impaired

She wakes to the sound of birds. Their chirping filters through the open window, soft, persistent and bright, like the sunlight she can no longer see. Morning has a rhythm now. It starts with sound, the shuffle of her husband's feet in the kitchen, the scrape of a chair against the floor. Then comes the smell. Eggs frying, butter melting, coffee brewing. She lies still, letting the scents fill the spaces where color and shape used to be.

Her husband brings breakfast on a tray, his steps steady, his voice warm. "Careful, the coffee's hot," he says, placing her hand on the smooth rim of the mug. She smiles, grateful for the small instructions that shape her world now. She doesn't need to see his face to know he's smiling back. She can hear it in the way he speaks, feel it in the way he touches her shoulder.

They are learning together. He labels the jars in kitchen with raised dots she can feel. She counts her steps to the bathroom, the kitchen, the garden. They laugh at their mistakes, at spilled salt and misplaced socks.

Sometimes, hopelessness creeps in, and she cries when she thinks he isn't watching, but he always knows. He holds her then, his silence louder than words.

She misses the sky most. The blue, the shifting clouds, the way the light changes at dusk. She tells him this one evening, her voice breaking. He doesn't answer right away. Later, he takes her hand and leads her outside. They sit in the cool grass, and he describes the sunset. "The sky is gold, with streaks of pink, like the roses in the garden," he says. She closes her eyes and listens, her chest heavy and full all at once.

Her world is smaller now, but it is not empty. It is filled with sound and scent, with texture and touch, with the steady presence of a man who loves her. Together, they piece it together, this new life, fragile and difficult, but still beautiful.

5. Longs to be free

She sits by the window, sunlight pooling at her feet like spilled gold, her reflection framed by the lattice of lace curtains. The girl in the glass is everything she's been told to be, neat, religious, the soul of modesty, and very untouchable.

Her skirt skims her knees like a curfew; her blouse hides the fullness of her bosom and her body. She wears decency like a veil, like a shroud, as if the world might crumble if she dared show too much of herself.

But beneath the fabric lies a smoldering ember, a yearning she can't confess. In her secret heart, she wants to be seen, not just seen, but desired. She dreams of men turning their heads, their gazes lingering like a flame.

She imagines their eyes tracing the curve of her shoulders, the dip of her waist. She wants to be more than an invisible virtue; she wants to make hearts race, to be the reason for a stuttered breath.

Her reflection changes when she lets herself imagine it. She is radiant, clad in a dress that glimmers like sin, its hem flirting with danger, its neckline plunging into a confidence she doesn't yet possess. Her lips are painted a red rebellion, her laugh—a melody that makes the world tilt toward her. In the dream, men look at her with intense hunger and admiration, and for once, she isn't afraid to meet their gaze.

The longing swells in her chest like a song unsung. She craves the power of her own beauty, the electric charge of stepping into a room and owning it. She wants to feel her own allure, to revel in it, to know that she is both art and artist.

But the walls of her upbringing press against her. She hears her mother's voice whispering of propriety, of shame. She feels the weight of expectations draped over her like an invisible cloak. Still, the ache persists, a quiet rebellion humming beneath her ribs.

Sometimes, late at night, she pulls her hair loose, and nude makes her way to the mirror.

And for a fleeting moment, she is the woman she longs to be—daring, seductive, alive. And though she always retreats before dawn, the ember glows a little brighter, waiting for the day she sets herself on fire.

6. When the World Sees

When the world sees your vulnerability,
like sharks, they can smell blood a mile away.
And they swarm around you
to tear, rip and devour
until
there's nothing left of you.

7. And I Am No Snitch

I won't breath a word
of all that transpired that night
Yeah, I know, it's all fucked up
I mean, I was there when you killed them
5 of your gang members you felt had betrayed you
You were hasty—sure—because after you had killed them
you discovered they had been set up
And they were your most loyal soldiers, actually
I helped you get rid of the bodies—quietly
And now they're sitting pretty at the edge of the sea, that is
whatever is left of them after the fishes have had their fill
Ain't no snitch
Snitches get stitches, man
I won't tell a soul
Your secret is safe with me
I'll take it to my grave…
not as if I'm planning on going to the grave anytime soon, well, maybe in the next forty years
Even when the cops came sniffing, I said nothing,
I held my ground,
and when their friends and relatives came asking,
I looked them in the eye
and told them we were equally perplexed and searching for them
Hell, we even put a hundred grand each
out for any information on their whereabouts
I won't tell how you dismembered their bodies and how
your plastic apron was stained with so much blood and gore
How I buried the aprons and shit
near that old warehouse and their clothes, too
I won't say shit, you feel me
I'ma keep it safe, not a word, homie

8. Love for Ghetto

For this our ghetto, where sun dey hot like fire
And life dey hustle us for corner, tire to tire
Love still dey shine like bulb wey no fit quench
For inside we wahala, e dey hold us like bench

She dey sell akara for junction, I dey push wheelbarrow
We no get plenty, but our heart dey glow like tomorrow
I go buy her groundnut even if my pocket dry
Her smile fit heal my hunger, I no go lie

Rain fit leak our roof, thunder fit clap
But when she dey my side, my soul dey nap
Her voice na my music, her laugh na my light
Even if darkness dey, she dey make am bright

Love for ghetto, no need big grammar
Na small-small things wey dey sweet like hammer
Na how we go share one plate of rice?
Or how she go tell me, "No worry, life go nice"?

So as I dey waka, I dey thank Baba God
Say even for dust, love dey grow like pod
For ghetto, love na hope, na strength, na power
E dey shine pass gold, e be ghetto flower

9. Nose on my body

And I smell so sweet
That you might be tempted to forget your nose
On my body

10. I Could Write You Into Forever

I could write a poem about you—
Fill its lines with the rhythm of your laughter,
Stretch it wide enough to hold all the years
Of memories we once shared,
And the quiet moments that slipped between us
Like whispers in the wind.

I could trace your name in the stars,
Hold the echo of your voice in my pen,
And make you a constellation—
A burning light where shadows dared to settle.
I'd draw you as you are and as I remember,
A tapestry of beauty, strength, and fragility.

With every verse, I'd lift you higher,
Turn your smallest steps into the dance of a goddess,
Carve a throne for you in the heart of my words—
A place where time cannot reach you,
Where loss is only a faint memory.

In my poem, you'd be endless,
Wrapped in the warmth of a love that never fades,
A living echo of all that was,
And all that still lingers.

I could write you into forever—
If only my words could keep you here.

The Adventures of Tom the Terror

Mike Ekunno

There was commotion when the gang of masquerades stormed the Udoka homestead on a 27th December pre-dawn raid. Like bees assailing an intruder, they crawled over the perimeter walls, taking time to avoid the spikes; attacked every green leaf, stripping trees bare; downed banana and plantain stems, and smashed the earthenware pots the family used to store water. The wrecking expedition went on all the time against the background wailing of a dozen of the masked spirits lamenting the desecration of their tribe in a war chant:

Nzogbu nzogbu!
Enyimba enyi!
Zogbue nwoke!
Enyimba enyi!
Zogbue nwanyi!
Enyimba enyi!

It was a riotous syncopation in which both the call and the response came in irregular staccato. The poultry of the household, not used to such a rude awakening, contributed to the bedlam in loud quacking.

Papa Udoka, the venerable head of the family, had been tipped off late the previous evening about what was in store. The antidote was to meet the mob at the gate with a live chicken in order to stave off the impending retribution, and then make sure the more valuable of moveable chattels were kept out of harm's way.

At the first inkling of the mob's approach that morning, Papa had accordingly dispatched an emissary to try to stanch the approaching hurricane at the entrance. That worked but only just. The heroics of having spirit beings levy distress would not be mollified on the altar of a chicken sacrifice or any other thing for that matter.

So the vanguard of the approaching hurricane snatched the sacrificial bird from the emissary's fearful hands, twisted its neck in a jiffy, and smashed it on the earth, where it lay writhing in death struggle. Now, one masked spirit made for the top of the perimeter fence, broke off a shard of the embedded broken bottle spike, and handed it over to the leader.

Grabbing the writhing bird again, the leader ran the shard across its twisted neck, and blood squirted in a V-formation. By then the rear guard of the mob had approached and the storming of the premises commenced.

The blitzkrieg ended as abruptly as it started. The masquerades withdrew, having extracted, if not maximum damage, such a symbolic slice of it as to warn any future delinquent bent on such abominable enterprise.

***

Thompson, who was responsible for the enterprise of desecrating the masquerade cult of the *Ifite* community, was yet sound asleep in his father's house. His offence belonged to the imaginary sphere because nobody in living memory had ever breached the taboo. Because of the rarity of its breach, the accompanying punishment had become fictional. Many said the culprit would be banished from the community. Others went from razing the homestead to his castration. The castration school was asked what would be done if a woman were the culprit.

Their debate remains ongoing. One thing on which all parties were agreed was the levying of distress and the fine. The offending family would have its livestock and moveable properties distrained to be redeemed with a fine.

The strong lobby from Papa Udoka had reduced the penalty to just the devastation witnessed that morning and a fine of ten yam tubers, a bottle of spirit, two gallons of palmwine, kolanuts and two live chickens, one of which was held out for ransom to the mob.

With the first crack of sunlight, neighbours descended on the Udoka homestead to find out what was amiss earlier. Among them was Donald, Tom's daddy and the first son of Papa Udoka. His morning routine since returning from America for the Christmas holiday with his family included the mandatory call on his father to greet, "*I putakwalu ula*?" "Have you survived sleep?"

Donald didn't have it coming—the sight that greeted him that morning at his father's *obi*. The distraining mob had tried his own home but couldn't breach its steel-gated, wire mesh-topped high walls. His father's *obi*, where the family house sat, was a low-hanging fruit, so the mob chose it in the alternative.

"What's all this, men?!" Donald asked of no one in his Yankee accent. Then he left the crowd outside and entered the *obi* where his father sat with some elders. "How dare they?" Don was livid as he took his seat. The rest of the seated sympathisers were relaxed but pensive. At their age, it's said that nothing the eye sees would warrant the shedding of blood as tears.

"You won't greet us?" It was from Don's uncle, Papa's younger brother.

Don immediately recovered his manners and greeted the elders—each by his cognomen, standing and moving round for a handshake and starting from his father:

"Ichie Chinyelugo."

"Egbe Ntu."

"Eke Nwe Ofia."

"Eze Ego."

"Eze Ego Oyibo," someone corrected him. The adjective clarified that it was the Whiteman's currency the man's kingship was about and not the country's diminished local currency.

The next elder's cognomen had escaped Don and he paused with both right palms locked in suspended animation of a handshake. "Remind me."

That plea brought on side comments about how American living had wiped away memory of home folks.

"Not that," Don's uncle came to his defence. "Ichie Gaskiya decided to bear a foreign nickname, that's why." Don immediately took the hint.

"Ichie Gaskiya," and the locked palms disengaged.

After he took his seat again, it was Eze Ego Oyibo who asked what led to this – the devastation staring at them on the forecourt. The question was directed at their host but it was his returnee son who answered.

"It is my fault, really," started Don before he went on to give the elders the backstory to what played out that morning.

Having arrived from Texas with his family for the Christmas holiday, Thompson, Don's second-grade son, was all fired up for his first African visit as a grown boy. He was a toddler the first time the family visited with his Chicago-born mother and Don's wife, Wendy.

In the one week they had been home before Christmas, Tom, The Terror had shown all how he earned that suffix to his name. Bulky for his seven years, he had warned his village playmates that he wasn't "fat" but "big." He looked like an uncle to his village playmates and the grapevine (out of earshot of his mother) said he was being fed America's human variant of broiler feed.

Full of Yankee energy, Tom relished the wonder of rustic living in the village with poultry and livestock roaming free.

Often, he set out to catch a chicken and ask him if he was brother to the one at KFC. On the chase, the hapless birds got flustered and would quack noisily, causing Mama, his grandmother, to plead with "Nwa Amelika" to leave her birds alone. At other times, he would try to ride a goat like a horse. The poor animal would flatten on the ground and bleat from the sheer heft, drawing Mama's lamentation on how "Nwa Amelika" would kill off her prize animals before she got a chance to sell them for Christmas. Every wakeful moment for Nwa Amelika had something intriguing to explore and not even the bumper-to-bumper policing from his aunty would leash his random instincts.

On Christmas Day, while his parents entertained guests, Tom's aunty, Chimamanda, readied for the day's sightseeing outing. Lots would be on display at the Ifite village square and no ripened damsel would miss out on the throng of eligible bachelors on the hunt.

There would be masquerades giving chase to giggling coquettes and having them screaming girlish screams. There would be dances and troupes—men, women, young, and old. Seduction would be hawked on curves and bulges from new Christmas wears that hugged full-figured bodies and litres of liquor will flow with gaiety all over the air.

It was in that zeitgeist that Chimamanda readied to leave home all dressed up. Tom got wind of the outing and clung to her like a leech intent on not being left behind. She tried to dissuade him by saying it was going to be a trekking outing, and nobody was ready to piggy-back any weight for tiredness.

Tom stuck to his guns. His mummy had to dress him up and ask the driver to take them.

"Chim," she called out to the departing Toyota Sienna, referring to Chimamanda by her own Americanised short form of the name, "I'm charging you with looking out for him." Her charge was to turn out prescient upon their return at 7:36 p.m.

Tom's head was covered in sand with one leg of his sneakers missing when they returned. He got smuggled by the driver through the rear door like a renegade.

When Chimamanda entered the porch to the lounge downstairs, Wendy was on the balcony and looking down, she asked, "Where's he?"

Chimamanda pointed to the rear, "Inside."

"So, how did it go?"

The nubile *agboghobia* collapsed on the porch in laughter, clapping her hands in wonderment. Her reaction piqued Wendy's interest and she came bounding downstairs to listen to the report of her son's escapades. Both women met inside the lounge and before Chimamanda could finish relaying the tales, Tom burst in naked and stripped for a bath. His daddy ran right behind and dragged him back to the bath where he ran water to scrub him down. While at it, he tried to debrief the little rascal.

"So, how did it go, Tom?"

"Very well, Dad. Hey, Dad, there were lots of Halloween costumes out there. Aunty says they're masquerades."

"O, yeah!"

"Those guys pack lots of canes."

"They're not guys, son. They're spirits. Alien spirits of our ancestors. They come visiting us humans during festivities like Christmas and Ede Aro."

"Oh wow! Ain't aliens like zombies, eh? We saw many boy-aliens too. Can children be ancestors, Dad?

"For sure. Ancestor kids are the children of the spirit world."

"They were dancing, Dad."

"Can you dance like them?"

"Yeah, Dad, if I got their costumes."

"I told you those are no costumes. That's how alien ancestors roll."

"You kidding me, Dad?! He was toweling his body at this time and paused to observe his daddy.

"No, son. I ain't kidding," Donald assured straight-faced.

After the adults of the house had had their fill bingeing on Tom's Christmas Day escapades, the family retired for the night. Up at his children's room, so designated in hope but hosting only the singular form for now, Tom wondered at his daddy's assertion about the alien ancestors. *How come ancestor zombies look so commonplace with nothing weird about them?* A dozen unanswered questions agitated his young mind until sleep came, for which he had no answer.

***

Boxing Day broke with its trademark languid airs. Beyond a few boxes of candy left for Tom by the spangled Christmas tree, there was not much to the day in the African tradition. There were lots of dishes to be done, empty bottles packed and food flasks to be returned to the owners who sent some Christmas hospitality in them.

In the laid-back apathy of the morning, Mama, Don's mother, stormed his son's house and made for the kitchen. She then proceeded to consolidate all the food gifts from well-wishers to the American returnees in one jute bag. Her mate, Mama Ngozi, had sent *ede*, the cocoyam in vegetable delicacy; another kindred family sent *abacha*; there were a couple of *onugbu* soup.

All went into the bag in one messy mélange. Wendy came into the kitchen while her mother-in-law was at it, standing transfixed in horror at the wasting of such hearty hospitality. She had especially looked forward to tasting the abacha which looked appetising enough.

"Ma-ma!" she let out.

Mama looked back and acknowledged her in her halting English, "I think you all have woken up well."

"O yeah. Thanks. And you … with Papa … and Mama Ngozi?"

"We slept well."

"I kept that one made from cassava flakes for myself, Mama," Wendy remonstrated.

"You want to die?"

"Oh no, Mama. Why would they want to poison us? How about all the stuff we sent out to people yesterday—would they also be trashed behind us?"

"Nwam, you not understand. They eat your food because you not poison them. You better pass them."

Wendy circled back from the kitchen and up the staircase to her husband in bed to complain.

"You won't get it," Donald muttered in resignation.

"And why the fuck is everyone saying the same thing?!"

By early afternoon, the Donald and Wendy household had recovered much of its spick and span looks thanks to the relentless cleaning, mopping, dusting and washing of Mama and Chimamanda.

As the morning began its handshake to noonday, the festive feel began to fester and unfurl like a full moon. Masquerades and dances got their acts on the road again. They moved from homestead to homestead displaying and being gifted money. Not a few had entered Donald's home because the gateman had been told to keep access open to them all in the spirit of the season.

Each group came expecting their share of the American dollars' largesse from their son and uncle who made good. Tom was having fun ingratiating himself as the go-between for the delivery of the cash tokens.

Using the good offices of his new status, he tried to satisfy his curiosity regarding his daddy's claims of Christmas Day. Some of the masquerades that came into their compound were adult ones that wielded canes. They would not flog the son of their benefactor, not to talk of an American boy with *Aje Bota,* a butter-eater, written all over him. So, Tom was allowed to be close-up with the masquerades while delivering their gift money.

He would gawk at each figure looking for tell-tale human features. The limbs appeared like human ones but their speeches were in a guttural accent.

After lunch, it was time again for festive sightseeing led by Chimamanda, who was a home-girl. This time, there was no question about whether Tom would join. His mother elected to join the party armed with a handicam. Together the party rolled out of the gate at 2:35 p.m.

Ifite village square on Boxing Day was a carnival on full throttle. Dances and masquerades which had spent Christmas doing the rounds of homes took their acts to town—literally. The season's festivities had coincided with the town's Ede Aro, a customary post-harvest celebration dedicated to the cocoyam. And 26th December happened to be the climax of the customary fiesta when all masquerades big or small, lay or esoteric, harmless or dangerous, congregated on the Ilo Aro square.

Indigenes of the more hinterland villages didn't miss the opportunity to come out and feast their eyes at Ifite, where they could get cold drinks at bars that had electricity from the national grid.

A fence of people skirted the arena of Ilo Aro. Sections of the fence would flow to and fro like water in a polythene bag when one masquerade or the other teased the spectators into a stampede.

Wendy had more than enough to record on her handicam. Donning aviator specs to douse the harsh sunlight and a T-shirt on a pair of jeans trousers, which she calls *pants* to Chimamanda's bemusement. The only thing that set her apart from the regular Ifite lady was the face mask she still wore. It was not for coronavirus. It was for the dust—a brown powder that settled on leaves, hairs, skins, cars and got inhaled silently. No true born of Ifite would use a face mask for the dust—for what?

Harmattan dust was par for the course. There was something else that set Wendy apart from the regular fare but that wasn't visible. She had to talk before you'd know she wasn't a local fowl; that she was a feed-fed breed and not just that—that she was Yankee with full options, not the pretend *been-to*.

Because of how people turned to gawk her when she spoke in a crowd, she always lowered her tone to a whisper while talking to Chimamanda or the driver. It was only her son who made her break that unconscious conditioning when she often had to yell, "Come back, Thompson!"

Tom the Terror was in his elements all the while and didn't disappoint. Nobody would accuse him of being pliant. They had banded together—he, his mum, and Chimamanda at the start, but with the stampedes and crowd presses at the approach of yet another of the nicely pesky masquerades, they soon drifted apart.

Only the driver hung around where the car parked. Chimamanda held on to Tom, who silently tried to confirm his daddy's assertion about the alien ancestral spirits.

Now at the square with its enlarged production, some of the masquerades looked so weird as to make him want to take Daddy's word for it. But then some others were quite pedestrian, with toes, human-like toes, peeping out of stockings. As if taking time out on his quandary, he brought out the chocolate bar that his mom had given him from the Christmas Tree boxes and freed his left hand from his aunty's clutch to unfurl the wrap. Unfurled halfway, a brown bar jutted out, and he took a bite.

One of the boy masquerades approached him,"*Nnaa, nyenum nwantonto, biko*," which means *Friend, do give me a little, please.*

It was in a hushed tone, not the guttural voice of the masquerade kingdom. It was in the same human voice of his playmates back at home who pelted him with Igbo, not minding his lack of understanding.

Tom didn't understand Igbo beyond *puta,* which means, *come out,* but he could guess what an outstretched hand and open palm meant for someone eating chocolate.

All around them, the adults were focused with necks straining for a glimpse of something. Tom looked at the solicitous ancestral alien boy, grabbed the raffia strands under his neck and yanked them up.

A bewildered face stared at him. Human face. Instantly, an alarm went up from the cheerleaders of the boy masquerade, *"Chai! O taa nmuo!"* meaning *he's betrayed a spirt* or *"Nwatakili-a-a etikpo isi nmuo!"* This child has wrecked the head of the spirit.

The pandemonium from the announcement had folks dashing to the scene while others ran away from there. The hapless ancestral spirit stood aghast, its cover blown, while the mob asked who the culprit was.

In the melee and before canes would start descending on bodies, Chimamanda gathered Tom's bulk in her two arms and ran.

Unlike Christmas Day when she wore heels, she was wearing flats, which aided her flight. Along their escape route, many were mobilising to the scene looking for who would have been responsible for such abomination. A double take told Chimamanda that their car would be useless by then, having probably been blocked by a gaggle of other cars.

She let her cargo down and dragged him to the road, where she flagged down a getaway *okada* motorbike. While the rider yet haggled the fare, she heaved Tom onto the back seat, then swung her left thigh over the seat behind him.

"Run, I say!" she yelled, and the Chinese machine jerked off on cue.

***

The case at the Ifite elders' council had dragged to mid-January over adjournments contrived by the elders' long throat for palmwine, which both parties to the dispute must supply on every adjourned date. It was not up to them to tell the plaintiff that hers was a wild bush fowl chase, an exercise in futility.

Mama Ngozi, Papa Udoka's second wife and co-wife to Donald's mother, was the plaintiff suing for her earthenware pots smashed by the distraining mob.

She claimed those were heirlooms from her own mother, gifted to her at her wedding. Her grouse was that the mob should have properly directed their retribution to the culprit or his grandmother and not to she, Nwamgbafor, who had no America-based son, let alone an iconoclastic American grandson who wrecked the *isi nmuo*.

Don and Wendy had gone to plead with her, offering to pay for the destroyed items, but she insisted on replacement with the exact clone.

When her docile husband was told, he asked whether she was the only one who didn't know that "a broken bottle (read earthen pot) has no mekwatalism."

Papa Udoka knew better than dragging the community's age-old customs before mortal judges. It was when the enraged woman asked why the mob left "that iron umbrella in their compound with which they watch what happens in heaven," referring to the satellite dish in Don's house, that the emissaries knew there was more to her hurt than broken pots. Everyone sat back and allowed her and her children to proceed to the elders' council.

Through the adjournments, it was Agwu, the head of the masquerade cult, who represented the defendants while Donald attended as a co-defendant representing his son—Thompson.

At the beginning, one elder had taken exception to Tom's absence in court and asked why.

"No, he's only a child," replied the presiding elder, a Justice of the Peace.

"That one that can impregnate a woman?" continued the objecting elder. The court erupted in laughter. Wendy was in court that day and asked her husband what the mirth was about.

"He said, Thompson is old enough to have a baby."

Wendy got up and left the courtroom.

As the family's departure date to the U.S. neared, the council had no choice but to wrap up its proceedings.

Judgment was fixed for the next Afor market day, which was three days thence. When it came, the judging elders assembled like the cast of a Nollywood epic.

The presiding judge started by saying, as non-corporeal entities, the masquerade spirits, being the visiting spirits of dead ancestors, could not be sued. Since they couldn't be sued, the matter of compensation for their actions became academic. But to address the inequity of destroying Mama Ngozi's pots when the offender was not her biological grandson, the judge warned that spirits carry their firewood askew and any passerby could be poked by its extensions, not minding the victim's innocence.

On that note, the case was dismissed without costs, the flow of palmwine during its pendency having been enough as costs. But the elder didn't say it like that.

Meet the Authors

Hannan Khan

Grand Prize Winner: ***Isn't Cooked is Cursed***

Hannan Khan, the grand-prize winner of the *Native Voices Award 2025* is a nefelibata, poet, and scholar of literature and linguistics from Pakistan. His work explores love, death, delirium, and relational complexity, tracing both the spoken and the unspoken. He writes across forms—haibun, ghazals, and speculative poetry—moving between intimacy and apocalypse. Drawn to dark thrillers, he reads with a forensic eye for the psychological and unpredictable. Poetry is his altar; fiction, his rebellion.

His work appears in *IHRAM Literary Magazine*, *Graveside Press*, *SpecPoVerse*, *Eye to the Telescope*, *Abyss & Apex*, *Failed Haiku*, *The Headlight Review*, and is forthcoming in *Notch Magazine*.

D. W. Simerly

1st Runner Up: *Lincoyer*

D.W. Simerly, the second-runner up of the *Native Voices Award 2025*, is a Mvskoke writer and teacher. Simerly earned his B.A. and M.A. in English literature from the University of North Alabama, where he serves as an adjunct English instructor. He enjoys writing horror, science fiction, and literary fiction. He currently lives in Florence, Alabama, with his fiancée and their cat, and continues to develop his voice across genres.

Mike Ekunno

2nd Runner Up: *The Adventures of Tom the Terror*

Mike Ekunno is the author of *Soul Lounge*, a collection of short stories, and winner of the inaugural *Harambee Literary Prize*. He works as a freelance book editor and speechwriter after leaving Nigeria's federal public service, where he served as a director in film regulation. His works have appeared in *The Republic*, *The Brussels Review*, *Mysterion, Rigorous*, *The First Line*, and within the winter 2025 issue of *Kinsman Quarterly Magazine.*

Aishik Chakma

The Last Thread

Aishik Chakma is a student from Bangladesh, currently living in Rangamati, and a member of the Chakma community. He is pursuing his college education with a strong interest in science, writing, and art. He writes short stories, poems, and essays reflecting on life, culture, and personal experience. In his free time, he enjoys painting, creating videos, and engaging in science activities. He hopes to use his writing to foster connection and deepen cultural understanding.

Alysha Brooks

A Nationless People

Alysha Brooks is a Native, dyslexic author and student living in British Columbia, Canada. Her first publication, "Dyslexia," appeared in *Dreamers Writing Collective* (2020), sparking her commitment to writing beauty from horror. This is her second publication in *KQ*'s *Native Voices* collections. Influenced by her grandfather, an Indigenous activist, her work engages themes of systemic oppression and resilience. You may follow her on Instagram @alyshalit.

Brian Jose Welch

Dark Moon

Brian Jose Welch is a writer from the Kettering District, Duncan, Trelawny, Jamaica. He attends the University of the West Indies and holds an associate degree in Arts and Social Sciences. A water sports advisor by profession, he writes poetry and short stories. His interests include reading, singing, dancing, comedy, traveling, and engaging online. He is committed to humanitarian work and community development.

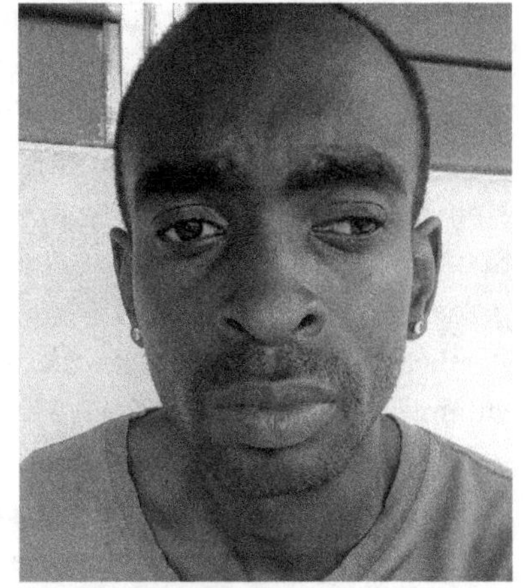

Chang Shih Yen

Two Sarawakian Poems

Chang Shih Yen is a a writer from Sarawak, East Malaysia. She graduated with first-class honors in English and Linguistics and holds an MA in Linguistics. Fluent in English, Chinese, Malay, Spanish, and Portuguese, she brings a global perspective to her work. She is the author of the short story collection *Around the World* (2022) and the children's book *Putra And His Silver Keris* (2023). She currently lives in New Zealand, where she continues to write and explore language and culture.

Douglas Perenara Johnston

A Dinner Engagement with Mister Top Hat and *Ram Raid*

Douglas Perenara Johnston lives in Oamaru, New Zealand, known as Janet Frame's "Kingdom by the Sea." Educated at the University of Otago, he is of Māori, Scottish, Irish, German, and Scandinavian descent. A graduate of NorthTec's Applied Writing programme, he weaves cultural identity into his work. He writes poetry, short stories, flash fiction, and creative nonfiction. His work appears in international journals, and he was a Top 6 Finalist for the *2024 Iridescence Award*.

Elaine Joy E. Degale

Moonflower

Elaine Joy E. Degale is an Afro-Pinay storyteller who moves between New York City and the sun-drenched shores of her native Philippines. Her travels and culinary explorations often inspire her short fiction. She is currently completing her novel, *Sunflower*. She also writes a weekly column for the *Philippine Daily Mirror* under the name "The Dreamweaver," where she reflects on arts, culture, and everyday life with imagination and insight.

Isha Jain

Ajji's Pineapple Cake

Isha Jain is a writer from India who believes that everyone and everything has a story to tell. Her work has been published in *Brown History*, *Mysticeti*, *riddlebird magazine*, and other platforms. She also writes on her Substack, *The Indian Story*, where she shares fiction and essays that explore culture, identity, and everyday life. Through her writing, she seeks to capture the depth and diversity of human experience.

Jay D. Falcetti

Inheriting Fear

Jay D. Falcetti (she/her) is a biracial Indigenous writer whose work is shaped by her upbringing on the Hualapai reservation. She holds degrees in Sociology and Criminal Justice & Criminology from Arizona State University, informing her interest in justice systems and human behavior. She writes speculative fiction that often explores themes rooted in her background. Her work has appeared in various magazines, and she is seeking representation for her fantasy novel.

Jordan Maison

Howl at the Moon

Jordan Maison is a Native American writer from the Ponca Tribe of Oklahoma. His love of storytelling began with film, leading him to study filmmaking in college. Over the past fifteen years, he has written extensively about film and entertainment, developing a strong critical voice. He brings that cinematic perspective into his own creative work, where he focuses on crafting compelling, story-driven narratives rooted in character and visual imagination.

Kirby Wright

Māmalahoa: Law of the Splintered Paddle

Kirby Wright is a writer born and raised in Hawai'i. His family land on Moloka'i once served as a vital breadbasket for Kamehameha's warriors as they prepared for their historic assault on O'ahu. Deeply connected to place and heritage, his work often reflects the histories, landscapes, and cultural legacies of the islands. Through his storytelling, he explores identity, memory, and the enduring significance of Native Hawaiian traditions.

Marc Apilado

Refreshment

Marc Apilado is a 20-year-old Filipino writer whose work explores themes of romance, self-discovery, and the beauty of everyday life. He views writing as a creative process of weaving narratives from ideas both internal and external, where possibilities feel endless. Through his work, he seeks to capture emotion and meaning in ordinary moments, inviting readers to reflect on their own experiences and connections to the world around them.

N.O. Gomez Flores

The Second First Woman

N.O. Gomez Flores is a Boricua artist born in Caguas, Puerto Rico, and currently living in San Antonio, Texas. He studied photojournalism at San Antonio College. A multidisciplinary creative, he paints, photographs, and writes, often drawing on the culture of his island. His work blends humor and fantasy to reflect both struggle and resilience. Influenced by artists like Rubén Blades and Douglas Adams, he brings a vibrant, imaginative lens to storytelling.

Sarah Martinez

The Memories of a Non-Rez Kid

Sarah Martinez is a writer and proud member of the Choctaw Nation of Oklahoma, raised in Wilburton, often called "the greener part" of the state. She studies at Brown University in Providence, Rhode Island, concentrating in anthropology and cultural studies. She has traveled extensively with Oklahoma Kids and the Girl Scouts of Eastern Oklahoma Travel Troupe. Her poetry explores identity, distance, and cultural heritage.

Sherry Caayupan

Heaven's Lips

Sherry Caayupan, the poet of "Heaven's Lips" is a writer from Davao City, Philippines. Though she came short of completing her college degree, she has continued to pursue her creative passions through writing. She enjoys exploring themes of love, humor, horror, and fantasy in her work. In addition to writing, she loves singing and gourmet cooking, bringing creativity and expression into many aspects of her life and daily experiences.

Solape Adetutu Adeyemi

The Heirloom

Solape Adetutu Adeyemi holds degrees in Microbiology and Environmental Management. She is an environmental sustainability advocate with experience across various roles in the food manufacturing industry. Her work has been published in *The New York Times*, *The Kalahari Review*, T*he Indianapolis Review*, *The Guardian*, and *Kinsman Quarterly's Iridescence* anthology. Solape can be reached at solapeadeyemi1@gmail.com

Tommy Cheis

Creator Will Never Tell

Tommy Cheis a Chiricahua Apache guide, medicine leader, and descendant of Cochise. After extensive travel and diverse encounters, he now lives with his horses in the Cochise Stronghold of Arizona. His stories have appeared in *Another Chicago Magazine*, *Puerto del Sol*, *Nonbinary Review*, *New Limestone Review*, *Collateral*, *ZiN Daily*, *After Dinner Conversation*, and over thirty other publications. A two-time *Pushcart Prize* nominee, his work was featured on the *CLMP* Reading List for Native American Heritage Month 2024.

Vernica Goel.

Silent Struggle

Vernica Goel was born and raised in Ambala, India. She is currently pursuing a Master's degree in Human Resource Management at XLRI Jamshedpur. A passionate writer, focused on nonfiction social justice, crafting reflective essays on inequality, human rights, and societal introspection. Her work amplifies marginalized voices and foster empathy-driven change. She enjoys watercolor painting and is a trained Kathak dancer who loves performing to Bollywood music.

www.ingramcontent.com/pod-product-compliance
Lightning Source LLC
LaVergne TN
LVHW020717110826
845149LV00012B/2310

* 9 7 8 1 9 6 2 1 2 1 6 3 7 *